THE MARKED WITNESS

Shadow Watcher, Book 3

VICKI HINZE

MAGNOLIA LEAF PRESS

THE MARKED WITNESS

© 2020-21 by Vicki Hinze

Published by Magnolia Leaf Press, Niceville, Florida
Print Edition ISBN: 978-1-939016-42-3
Digital Edition ISBN: 978-1-939016-41-6
First Edition 2020, by agreement with the author, Murder and Mistletoe
Printed in the USA
10 9 8 7 6 5 4 3 2

THE MARKED WITNESS

CHAPTER ONE

Summerland
Hitch, Alabama
Monday, December 21, 1:30 PM

Sam Holt tugged off his ball cap then sprawled on the sofa, half-watching a rerun of the season's first college football playoff between Oregon and Ohio State. The national championship was on the line but being a diehard, self-proclaimed Alabama redneck and Crimson Tide—*Roll Tide Roll*—fan, he didn't have a dog in this race. That, plus the fact he and the rest of the world already knew the winner, made the game good snooze TV.

After the all-nighter he'd pulled running background for Tim's latest PSC—Personal Security Consultants—mission, a firm Sam and his partners owned, he needed a power nap. Settling in, he closed his burning eyes and sank into a deep slumber.

The piercing shrill of a ringing phone roused him. The caller lacked a priority call ringtone so, without opening his eyes, Sam snagged his phone and mumbled, "If this is a telemarketer or a political call, spare yourself and hang up now."

"Sam? It's Jaycee Cole. I, um, I hope I'm not disturbing you . . .."

Jaycee. The woman he wanted but could never have. His eyes snapped open. Sam hadn't seen or heard from her since she and her daughter, Lizzie, had left nearby Seagrove Village, Florida, going on six years ago. His heart jackhammered and hollowed, and the too-familiar ache of letting them go flooded in. He lived with plenty of rough times. That came with the territory for Shadow Watchers. Spies who spy on spies made dark situations routine in daily life. His post-military work with PSC was the same. Yet watching Jaycee and Lizzie leave their village home for their undisclosed second relocation in witness protection had nearly killed him.

Had to be done. No choice.

That was the sorry truth. He'd known it then, but he'd also believed, with time, missing them would get easier. It hadn't. Then he'd hoped he'd get better at coping with them being gone. His partners had said he would, but that hadn't worked out for Sam either. Every year that passed without them seemed like the hardest one yet—even knowing that if he wanted them to live, and he definitely wanted them to live, they had to go. Jaycee and Lizzie not being in his life hurt, but the thought of him being in a world they were no longer in . . . that brought him more pain than Sam could bear.

"Are you doing okay, Sam?"

Without them? How did he answer that? "Day by day. You?"

"Day by day." Her sigh crackled through the phone. "Honestly, no. No, I'm not okay."

The imagined images of her and Lizzie being happy that kept him functioning, shattered. His jaw clamped down. "Why not?"

"Sorry. I need a minute." Her voice faltered. "This is even harder than I expected."

"Okay." The list of possible wrongs exploded in his mind. Before they'd met, Jaycee had been a young widow with an infant, working as a government contract negotiator with access to a system in development that would change modern warfare. NINA, Nihilists in Anarchy, an infamous terrorist organization and also PSC's archenemy, wanted it. Jaycee blew the whistle. NINA blew up her car and her house. Personal safety required she and Lizzie enter witness protection and relocate.

Command followed the money on the project and discovered Bradley Warrington, Jaycee's boss, had cut a deal with NINA and pointed the terrorists to Jaycee, a witness who knew too much. The deal included Jaycee never testify against Warrington or his powerful and corrupt friends. On Warrington's indictment, NINA assigned a mid-level operative, John Ranger Craft, to assassinate her. But en route to execute the kill order, Craft's small plane reportedly went down. No evidence of the crash or him had been found. Craft was presumed dead and eventually Jaycee testified, Warrington was convicted and, aided by his corrupt and powerful friends, he was sent to a minimum security, country-club prison.

Even now Sam continued to monitor all channels, and there had been absolutely no sign of John Ranger Craft. Most likely, he'd not dared to refuse the NINA assassination assignment, but he had seen the wisdom in not executing a joint assassination order for NINA and Warrington against a witness under Command's high-threat protection. Classic *between the rock and the hard place* position for Craft. Out of options, he had elected to tap out, probably faking his death and living large on some remote island far, far away.

"How is she?" Sam asked Jaycee. She would know he was talking about Lizzie.

"Growing up too fast."

Without him.

But she was alive. They both were . . . For the thousandth time in the past month, he wished he had asked her to stay, to marry him. But that was a selfish road he hadn't dared to travel.

Back then, because NINA never left loose ends, Command had insisted Jaycee relocate under a new identity to Seagrove Village, Florida, the home of NINA's worst nightmare and archenemy, PSC. Since NINA had issued standing orders to everyone in its organization to avoid both PSC and the village, sending Jaycee and Lizzie to it was their best and her safest possible option. A good call in Sam's opinion.

But the order didn't hold.

Rogue NINA operatives defied the direct order—PSC already had inflicted an enormous amount of damage on the organization —and made a second attempt though another village venue to get the system. Not a huge shock because, if successful, the system would make a fortune on the black-market and NINA would recoup a lot of the revenue PSC had cost them. Finding Jaycee in Seagrove Village had been an added bonus.

NINA never forgets or makes idle threats. Hadn't then, didn't now. Operatives came after her again in a dangerous clash where Sam and his team of PSC partners had successfully interceded and saved Jaycee and Lizzie's lives for the second time.

Every NINA operative on the planet had already been after Sam and his partners. Typical risks for those who routinely pulled high-priority operations for government entities that didn't exist on paper. Of course, NINA retaliated at every opportunity, just not in Seagrove Village. PSC's work was always essential to national security and extremely risky for the partners, their family members, and even people about whom they cared. Sam cared about Jaycee and Lizzie and, to get to Sam, NINA would have killed them both for sport. That left no choice but for Jaycee and Lizzie to relocate —again.

"Sam, I'm sorry. I am disturbing you." Remorse riddled Jaycee's voice. "You were resting, weren't you?"

"You always disturb me, but only in the best possible way." The fissure of fear opened wider in Sam's stomach and spread on a tingle to his limbs. What was he thinking? He cleared the fog from his mind. Jaycee calling him? This had to be bad news. For her to contact him, it had to be the worst kind of bad news. He sat up straight, planted his feet firmly on the floor and braced for it. He couldn't let her not answer his question. If she wasn't okay, he needed to know why not. "Straight answer, Jaycee. Are you two okay?"

"No, Sam." Jaycee's voice cracked and she paused, composed herself and then spoke in a whispered rush. "We're not."

He waited but she didn't say anything else, so he prodded her. "What's wrong?" Was she hurt? Lizzie? His heart slammed against his ribs. He pulled his ball cap on, dragged it low, shielding his eyes. It intensified his focus.

"We're not hurt. Not yet, anyway. But I'm afraid I need your help again, and I need it now." She groaned. "Sorry. That sounded melodramatic even to me. I do need your help, and I really am sorry, but I'm struggling with this. We've been so careful, and yet . . . Please, just bear with me and give me another second to collect my thoughts. Is that all right?"

"Sure." Jaycee was suppressing her emotions not collecting her thoughts, so he held his tongue. She had always been self-reliant, competent and rarely asked anyone for anything if not asking was humanly possible. If she said she needed help, she *really* needed help. What the first incident hadn't proven, the second one had.

That second one haunted him, asleep and awake. After the first incident resolved, NINA assumed PSC had taken out Craft and had left Jaycee alone. But a stone-cold killer, its Costa Rica connection, Diego Vargas, who had been promised the system and had made a verbal agreement with a buyer for it, wasn't happy about not getting it. To save his reputation with the buyer, he'd blamed Jaycee. He didn't just want her dead, he wanted revenge.

To get both, Vargas ordered Jaycee and Lizzie abducted. They were snatched and shipped to Costa Rica, where Vargas's revenge had made them part of a human hunt.

Dark, vivid memories flashed through Sam's mind. Memories of learning Jaycee and Lizzie's predicament. Of the partners reacting swiftly, getting down there and interdicting them, but Sam couldn't forget what a close call it had been. Another twenty-four hours and he would have been too late.

"Thanks for your patience," Jaycee said, now sounding calm and collected. "I need your help, Sam."

Three times, she'd asked. She was terrified. "Anything, anytime, anywhere. Goes without saying." Sam reminded her of his promise. "What do you need?"

"I hate to ask." She paused.

"I know. Do it anyway," he urged her.

Her breath hitched then crackled, and a distinct tremble roughened her voice. "It's so close to Christmas and I'm sure you have plans."

"What do you need, Jaycee?"

"Would it be possible for you to come here?"

"Yes," he said immediately. For her safety, he had no idea what her name was now or where she and Lizzie had gone or been since leaving. But none of that mattered. He'd trek to the ends of the earth for either of them. "Just tell me where you are."

"Arlington."

That stunned him into stroking his beard. Like Sam, Jaycee preferred small-town rural life. Or she had. "You're in Virginia?" Maybe she'd changed? He couldn't see that happening. Not for her or for Lizzie.

"Good grief, no." Jaycee sounded genuinely mortified. "Arlington, Alabama."

"Seriously?" An hour away. All this time and they were just an hour away. That stunned him, but it made a lot more sense. He had spent many a night wondering where they were, certain Jaycee would never go back to upstate New York, where she'd lost her husband when Lizzie had been an infant. Back then she'd used her real name, Jaycee Cole. She hadn't become Sue Ellen Montgomery until witness protection and Seagrove Village.

If he were alive, John Ranger Craft could be after her again, Sam supposed, but six years and not a single sighting made it highly unlikely. Warrington or his powerful friends? Possible. Maybe someone from the Costa Rica connection? Diego Vargas had run NINA operations for Costa Rica and the entire continent. Also possible.

Jaycee reclaimed Sam's attention. "Arlington is northeast of Mobile, not too far from Selma," she said, giving him a frame of reference.

"I'm familiar with Selma." He just never thought she'd be that close to Summerland, his family's spread in Hitch. "Do I need to bring friends?"

"I wish I could tell you. I just don't know, and it might not be safe to say too much on the phone." She seemed confused, torn and devastated all at once. "You know, maybe this isn't a good idea," she said. "If anything happened to you because of me, I'd never forgive myself."

That sealed it. It was bad, the most dangerous kind of trouble. He needed threat specifics—soonest. Jaycee was in protect mode. If he wanted to know what was going on anytime soon, he'd have to get details from Lizzie. The kid took blunt and direct to Space Force levels a hundred percent of the time. "Let me speak to her."

A pause, then when Lizzie spoke, her voice echoed, like she was far away. He presumed she was speaking to her mother. "You're talking around the problem, Mom. At this rate, it'll take you all night. Give me the phone. I can handle this in three words."

Lizzie clearly got the phone, then said, "Sam?"

Her voice was older to his hungry ear. But it would be. Lizzie was nearly sixteen now, not the ten she'd been when he'd last seen her. "Hi." What was going on there? He hauled himself upstairs and started tossing gear into a duffle bag. Whatever the problem was, it had the unflappable Jaycee rattled to the core and Lizzie even more serious than usual. Certainty of danger drove into him like nails. He needed to move.

"You said three words." Jaycee reminded Lizzie from the background.

"I've got to be sure it's Sam first." Lizzie went silent while Jaycee mumbled something he didn't catch, and then Lizzie spoke into the phone to him. "It's you, right? Promise."

Lizzie unsure of him, of her own ears? She'd always been as opinionated as a heart attack and known her mind immediately. "It's me. I promise." He grabbed a spare set of shoes. "Fishing on the pier. Doing cannonballs into the river at the bend. We're the keepers of secrets."

"Like what?"

He pulled on his boots. "You drove my lawn tractor over your mother's favorite flower bed. I took the hit, but you fessed up. She was pretty peeved at us both."

"Madder than when I drove your monster truck off the trails to the lake?"

"Oh, yeah. It took us a week, working sunup to sundown, to fill the ruts, too." He nearly smiled. She'd worked right alongside him. "It's me, half-pint." Back then, he and Lizzie had a code word for imminent danger, but would a sixteen-year-old Lizzie even remember that?

Lizzie exhaled a relieved gush. "Purple People-Eater."

She remembered, all right. Sam's breath caught, sharp and fast and his heart skipped a full beat. "Where?"

She gave him GPS coordinates. He committed them to memory, zipped up his duffle and swung it off the bed, then headed down the stairs. "Are you two safe right now?"

"We're in hiding."

Not in the house. Somewhere else. "I'll be there in an hour." It'd take longer to fly than to drive. "Can you stay safe where you are for that long?"

"I wanted to go sit in the police station. Considering stuff, Mom says we're safer here. She's totally right."

Jaycee didn't want to involve the local police. He understood that need to stay below the radar, but that too was a warning.

Her instincts were honed—he trusted them. Otherwise, she'd have been dead long ago. Still, Sam was curious. "What do you say?"

"We're good for now," Lizzie said. "Anything changes, we'll move to a new secure location and let you know."

"I'll stay on the phone with you." He stuffed his wallet into his pocket, shoved his arms into the sleeves of his brown duster coat, traded his baseball cap for his hat, then grabbed his truck keys.

"No. Too long on the phone. Someone could hear. When you get there, call. We'll come."

Lizzie was thinking, and the fear etching into her voice had his stomach in knots. "All right. Anything happens, you call me." He locked up, hustled to the truck and cranked the engine. "I mean anything."

"Promise. You're on speed-dial."

Sam stomped the gas and left a trail of churning dust all the way to the main road. "I'm on my way." He adjusted the rearview mirror. "Half-pint, just how serious is this?" She'd respond with a number from one to five.

"A solid ten."

CHAPTER TWO

1:50 PM

Heading north in his truck, Sam phoned to let Bob, the Summerland foreman, know he'd be away, then disconnected and issued a second voice command. "Call the office."

A long moment later, Nick answered the phone. "PSC."

That surprised Sam. "I thought you and Elle were on tour in Hamburg, or something." Nick was married to the superstar singer, Elle.

"We got back Saturday." Nick still sounded a little jet lagged. "How are things on the estate?"

Since Sam had inherited Summerland two years ago, Nick used *estate* to needle Sam. What true Southerner used the word estate to describe his spread? He'd intended to talk to Mark or Joe, the kings of connections in all places, but Nick was an expert with computers. The best anywhere. "I need Mark, too," Sam said, nixing the small talk. "Now."

"You okay?"

"Yeah, buddy."

A beat later, Mark got on the secure line. "We're all here, Sam, and you're on speaker. What's up?"

By all, Mark meant Nick, Tim, Joe and himself. They, with Sam, comprised the partners of PSC. And it was best Nick had summoned the team, Sam decided. Save Mark the time of repeating everything to the others. "Jaycee is in trouble. I don't know what kind yet, but I'm on my way to her now."

"Lizzie okay?"

"She's with her mother," Sam said. "Jaycee says they're not hurt. But they're in hiding away from their home."

"You need backup," Tim said.

"Not yet," Sam told him.

"Lizzie give you a ranking?" Joe asked.

Leave it to him to be tuned in to females. Young or old, they gravitated to him and always had. "A solid ten."

"But she never ranks anything above a five."

Nick was right. She never had. "She's nearly sixteen now," Sam said. "I need to assess for myself."

"She could be going through that drama phase, but this is Lizzie," Joe reminded Sam. "She doesn't do drama, not even when it's warranted."

Sam gritted his teeth and passed a slow-moving sedan with a bumper sticker that read *Live free or die*. "I know that, Joe." Sam elevated his voice. The shout wasn't due to anger but fear. She'd tagged the Costa Rica incident a four. Armed men chasing her and her mother through the woods, and she'd tagged that a four. He'd ranked it a ten. Still had nightmares about it. What would it take for Lizzie to rank anything a ten? He didn't dare to imagine.

Focusing on the practical, Mark cut to the chase. "What do you need first, Sam?"

"Check on Jaycee's John Ranger Craft," Sam said.

"He's dead," Tim said. "Plane crash, remember?"

As if he could forget. Sam sought patience. "A lot of NINA operatives have been dead and come back to fight another day."

"Sam's right but, Sam," Nick said, "you already monitor him."

Sam gritted his teeth. "Maybe I missed something. If there's been any activity, I want to know it."

"You got it," Nick said.

"Run an update on Vargas, too."

"Who?" That from Tim. "Clarify."

"Diego Vargas, the NINA Costa Rica connection."

"You reported him KIA in Costa Rica," Nick reminded Sam.

"We're not running just ghosts," Sam said. "Vargas was killed in action. We all saw it. But he ran all of South America's operations. NINA didn't just let their interests go fallow because Vargas was neutralized. Maybe his successor picked up with Jaycee where Vargas left off."

"I've got this one," Joe said.

Sam was glad to hear it. Joe knew everybody everywhere. He would save them a lot of time.

Jaycee's old boss, the man responsible for her troubles, Bradley Warrington, could be stirred up. "Check on Warrington, too." Powerful and once highly positioned made him dangerous even behind bars. Sam stroked his beard. "Make sure he's still in jail and snag a listing of who's been to see him or called." If another assassin or NINA operative was after Jaycee, one of those related incidents was most likely the root source. The sooner Sam knew which one, the better.

"This new trouble could be unrelated to the old," Mark said.

"Could be." Sam agreed. "Lizzie wasn't specific. Neither was Jaycee. But having the current status on all of them could help me eliminate them."

"We're all over it, Sam," Mark told him. "Man, I am so sorry about this."

"Why are you sorry?" Sam asked. If Mark had known anything about this and not told Sam . . .

"I'm sorry they're still having to live with these jerks wrecking their lives." Mark said the words, but the mumbled agreement of the others echoed clearly in the background. They'd thought a lot of Jaycee and Lizzie, too. "First this NINA and Warrington, then

Craft, then Costa Rica and Vargas, and now more? It just isn't right."

Tim grumbled. "She's like a trouble magnet."

"Careful, buddy." Sam let the warning to tread lightly ride on his words.

"No, Sam. Sorry. I meant she never asked for any of this. She's just a witness, doing what's right, and it's marked her for life." Tim sighed, then added, "I wish this stuff would stop and she and Lizzie would catch a break."

"Isn't that the truth?" Joe smoothed some calm over the peace. "Luckily, we got to them in time in Costa Rica."

Sam agreed on all fronts. Yet another close-call memory flashed through his mind. The thick woods of the forest. Hot. Dark. Sultry. The team frantically scrambling to get into position, then waiting for the captors to cut Jaycee and Lizzie loose. They did, and the hunt was on. Jaycee and Lizzie were the prey. They ran, the hunters waited, chomping at the bit for the signal to give chase. Diego Vargas jumped the gun, and Sam took him out, then searched and finally spotted Lizzie peeking out from behind a tree. He intercepted her and Jaycee. The team surrounded and extracted them, then got them safely back to the States. Lizzie had clung to Sam the entire flight. Her thin arms trembling. "We did," Sam said. Barely in time, but they'd made it. His heart beat faster.

"Too close for comfort," Joe said. "If they were here, it'd be easier to protect them. Just sayin', bro."

Sam squeezed the steering wheel. "They were in Seagrove Village when Vargas snatched them. Remember?"

"True, and living here under different identities," Joe conceded. "That's on us. Thinking we had them all in custody and the village was off-limits."

A truth that gnawed at Sam every day of his life. He braked for a stop sign, waited for a woman pushing a toddler in a stroller to cross the street. "We were wrong."

"Yeah, we were," Mark said.

The steering wheel slicked under Sam's tight grip. "And Jaycee and Lizzie nearly paid the price for that with their lives." Who was he kidding? They could still be paying.

"Sam," Nick interrupted. "There's been no activity on John Ranger Craft. You didn't miss anything. And none on Bradley Warrington. The good news is there isn't likely to be any on him anytime soon."

Curious. Sam passed a firehouse. Four firemen were washing the truck. "Why is that? Is he dead?"

"Not yet," Nick said. "Three months ago, Warrington killed a guard and two cellmates. The warden yanked him out of the country-club facility and shipped him to a maximum-security prison. He hasn't seen a soul since the transfer."

Maximum security had degrees. "Which one?"

"Alcatraz of the Rockies."

"ADX Florence in Colorado." Sam absorbed that. The country-club warden hadn't messed around, sending Warrington to the supermax prison situated miles from anywhere and reputed to be the most secure prison in the world. Command had to have weighed in on that move, warning Warrington, his corrupt associates and NINA they'd had enough and were done playing around. No one got in or out of that bleak fortress uninvited. "You're sure he's had no visitors?"

"Yes. None," Nick said. "No interaction with other prisoners, and no phone calls made or received either."

"For how long?"

"Since he was moved there, September 17th. Actually, he's had no outside contact whatsoever. Not even with his lawyer."

Joe chimed in. "There's nothing to report, Sam. I've checked everywhere. No one has any activity on Jaycee or Lizzie or their aliases Sue Ellen and Megan Montgomery."

"You checked on Vargas associates, too."

"I did, bro," Joe assured him. "His replacement is paranoid of us. Ordered his people to avoid by all means necessary provoking another visit from us to their country."

"Works for me," Mark said, stepping in. "Anything else you need, you let us know, Sam. We're on operational standby."

"Thanks, guys." Sam slowed to let a bicyclist turn the corner without crowding him.

As he reached to disconnect the call, he heard Nick. "Lizzie never ranks anything a ten."

"Truth, that." Joe agreed. "Like I said, she tagged Costa Rica a four. Being hunted down like that—"

"Sam's well aware of it all," Mark cut in. "He's got this. Whatever he needs, we're there. Get the chopper gassed up and gear loaded . . ."

Mark was still spitting out orders when the line went dead.

Sam's big body shook. He prayed Mark proved right and he did have this. He could not fail Jaycee and Lizzie. Not and live with himself.

CHAPTER THREE

Arlington, Alabama
Monday, December 21, 2:47 PM

According to the GPS, Sam had arrived. The narrow road had a shell lot near a pond where a couple cars could pull off and park, but trees and weeds and water were the only things around. Were they hiding in the woods? He scanned but didn't spot so much as a trail. "Call Jaycee," he issued the voice command.

When she answered, he said, "Waiting."

"In your truck?" Jaycee asked.

"It's a new one," he said. "Same color."

Minutes later, a sleek SUV pulled onto the shell lot and stopped beside him. Sam got out and rounded the backend.

Lizzie barreled out of the SUV, ran and launched herself into Sam's arms. She hugged him so tightly, a knot rose and stuck in his throat.

"I missed you so much, Sam." She squeezed him harder, burying her nose in his neck, her whole body shaking.

Jaycee slid out and closed the door. Still petite, still slender, but her hair wasn't sun-washed blonde like Lizzie's anymore. It was a deep auburn that the sun danced in and set her piercing blue eyes ablaze. Not even the dark shadows beneath them and the haunted look in them could dull her sparkle. The sight of her still left him breathless.

"Thank you for coming." She mouthed the words and tugged the hem of her soft white sweater down on her faded jeans.

She was glad to see him. Or maybe just relieved. Over Lizzie's shoulder, he winked at her, then told Lizzie. "I missed you too, half-pint."

She reared back and looked at him, her expression serious. "You're still big as a mountain. I thought since I've grown so much, you'd be smaller, but you're not."

He nearly smiled. "Sorry." Being six-six and broad, he often got that kind of reaction . . . and complaints in the field that he made too huge a target.

"Just an observation." She patted his beefy arms. "I'm glad, actually. You look the same, except your hair's longer and not as red." She lifted a curly lock brushing his shoulder, then touched his face. "And your beard's shorter. I like it trimmed." She looked back at her mother. "Don't you like it trimmed, Mom?"

"I do." Jaycee folded her arms across her stomach. "Still looks like he stepped out of an 1800s history book." She nodded. "You always have loved that time."

"My favorite era," Sam said, then swiveled his gaze to Lizzie and grunted. "You've shot up about a foot, but you still look like Lizzie." He cocked his head. There were many changes, but from ten to nearly sixteen, there should be. "You sitting on your hair these days?" It was pulled back in a ponytail that hung low on her back.

"Not yet." She shrugged. "Can't say I'm extra fond of it this long, but it keeps my head warm in the winter." She smacked a kiss to his cheek and squeezed his arms, motioning him to put her down.

He gingerly set her to her feet on the ground, then held out his arms to Jaycee.

She walked into them and wrapped her arms around his waist,

then pressed her cheek to his chest. "I'm so glad you're here," she whispered into his coat at his chest. "I hope I don't regret calling you, but . . ."

"I'm glad, too." He sensed her fear. "I've missed you, Jaycee."

She looked up at him and pressed a butterfly kiss to his chin. It was as high as she could reach unless he bent down. He kicked himself that he hadn't. Even Lizzie was taller than her mother now. Jaycee topped out at five feet, but anyone testing her shouldn't forget dynamite comes in small packages.

Backing away, Jaycee scanned the road, then the woods. "We better go. We're exposed out in the open like this."

"I'm riding with Sam." Lizzie headed for the passenger's door of his truck. "That's okay, right?"

"That's fine." Jaycee nodded.

"If she gets lost," Lizzie explained, "I can get you there and she'll catch up."

That wasn't happening. He wouldn't be letting Jaycee out of his sight. At the SUV, Sam opened the driver's door. Jaycee slid in and he closed it behind her. She cranked the engine and waited for him to get in the truck.

He took to his seat. "Buckle up, Lizzie."

"I am buckled," she said. "I love this truck almost as much as your monster truck—for taking on the road, I mean." Her eyes sparkled. "Is there anything it doesn't have on it?"

"Nothing they offer." He chuckled. "I went a little overboard." The guys had teased him for a week.

"Well, I love it." She looked his way but didn't crack smile.

So serious. She always had been, but he'd hoped . . . "So, where do we go?"

"Just follow Mom." Lizzie went quiet.

Fifteen minutes later, he hadn't seen the first house, the first business or any kind of structure. Even for Jaycee, this wasn't rural, it was remote. Was she still running that scared? Must be. The knots in his gut wound tighter.

"Sam, I gotta know. Why did you come?" Lizzie asked. She leaned against the door, pivoted her head and frowned at him.

"I'll always come for you two. You know that." He lifted a shoulder. "I promised."

She nodded. "Anything, anywhere, anytime."

His parting words to her and her mother. "That's right."

"For how long?"

He met her gaze. "Long as I'm drawing breath, half-pint."

"You haven't married anybody that'll get upset?"

That's what she really wanted to know. "No." How could he do that, even with the guys urging him to move on. His heart wasn't his to give to anyone else. It'd left with them.

She took that in, and a layer of worry slid from her face. "You still love us."

"Love ain't a water spigot you turn on and off, half-pint."

"It sure ain't, Sam."

She, at least, still loved him, too. But Jaycee? That was another matter entirely and he had no idea.

Before he could probe Lizzie on that, she pointed straight ahead. "Right around this bend, there's a mailbox on the left. Careful or you'll miss it. Mom does half the time, so if she goes further, don't follow her."

He steered out of the bend. "I see it." Two muddy ruts led deep into the woods. Jaycee made the turn. Sam followed.

"I couldn't give you the address. I'm not allowed to speak it over the phone. Safety measure." The truck rocked and Lizzie clasped the door and held on.

Jaycee had a lot of safety-measure rules. He'd taught her many of them. "Pretty long trail."

"The cabin's just ahead."

Just after the words left Lizzie's mouth, the cabin came into view. Made of logs, stained deep brown, it had a wide front porch. Four wooden rockers were on it and a porch swing hung on one end. "You gonna to tell me what's going on anytime soon?"

"I promised not to talk about it until we're in the cabin. Sorry." She shrugged. "I would tell you anyway because we're keepers of secrets, but Mom's been so scared. I think if she gets one more shock, she might break." Lizzie licked at her lips. "I—I can't risk breaking her."

If Jaycee were going to break, it would have happened long ago. But Lizzie being attuned to her mother was a good thing, so he didn't mention it. "That seems sensible, to me." Being sensible had always been important to Lizzie.

"Everybody has limits, right?"

"Indeed, they do." He gently squeezed her hand. "Let's see if we can fix whatever this is so you both can rest easy again." He would fix it or die trying, and that was a fact.

Lizzie's chin trembled and her eyes shone overly bright. "That would be the best thing ever, Sam." She looked as weary as Jaycee did haunted.

Seeing them like this nearly yanked his heart out of his chest. "We'll find a way to make it right, so you quit worrying."

A tear dripped to her cheek, and she nodded. "Won't be easy."

"Never is, but we manage. You remember how?"

"We keep at it, using our heads. We don't give in to fear. And we never quit."

She'd ticked them off on her fingers, just like he had when he'd first told them to her. That put a lump in his throat. "That's right."

Surprise flitted across her face. "You didn't say, 'Dang right'."

He grunted. "I got tired of jalapeño juice getting slipped into my iced-tea."

"Nora especially did take exception," Lizzie said. "Cussing is a sign of a weak mind."

Nora, the elderly village mother who took in all strays and called the PSC team *her boys* had said so a million times. And no one dared to dispute her on anything. They'd have to fight the whole village. Seemed Lizzie remembered every single thing from her life there. He hoped that was a blessing not a curse. Parking in the clearing, he cut the engine and they got out of the truck.

Already at the door, Jaycee fumbled her keys. Her hand was shaking. Looking beyond the clearing, he saw a path to his left. He spotted no flowers, no gardening supplies, and nothing personal. That just wasn't like Jaycee. "How long have you been here?"

"About two years." Jaycee turned the knob and opened the door, then stepped inside.

"Since Seagrove, we travel light," Lizzie whispered as she passed Sam.

The gathering room opened into a bright and airy kitchen with a breakfast bar and a long table beyond it that faced windows with the view of a clearing and the woods beyond it. Nothing but trees and grass were in his line of sight.

Lizzie walked straight to the coffeemaker and put on a fresh pot.

"Sit down, Sam." Jaycee motioned to the long table. "Oh, sorry. The coat rack is by the door."

He shrugged out of his long brown duster and then placed it on a hook. It hung right between Jaycee and Lizzie's. He pulled off his hat and hooked it atop it. The look of his things hanging with theirs made him feel good.

Then he turned and spotted Jaycee, moving methodically through the cabin, checking every window lock and inside every closet. "Does she do that all the time?"

"Every time we leave the house." Lizzie sat down at the table. "Not that we've had trouble with intruders or anything."

He was glad to hear that. But out in the middle of nowhere, he suspected nobody could find them. "Safety measure." He tilted his head to a flight of stairs. "What's up there?"

"Two more bedrooms and another bath. Our bedrooms are down that hall." She hiked her chin toward it. "What you see, plus a laundry room, two bedrooms and two baths are down here."

"It's a nice cabin."

Lizzie nodded. "We've got a hundred acres. The cabin is nearly dead center. There's a pond, too. It's not as big as Summerland's, but it's got brim and bass in it."

She still liked to fish. He remembered teaching her to bait a hook. "Betting there's a lot of game in these woods." Sam looked out the windows. Safe bet.

"I see deer all the time. Wild turkey, too." Lizzie almost grinned. "The deer ate all Mom's flowers. She was not happy. Plowed up all the flowerbeds." That declaration was offered with a suitable eye roll Sam understood only too well.

"I wondered about that. Hard to picture your mom in a house without flowers planted everywhere in the yard."

"Just another thing we have to live without," Lizzie told him. "That's what she said."

"Crying when she said it?" he asked.

"Oh, yeah." Lizzie went dark and serious again. "She doesn't know I know it, but she cries a lot now."

He especially hated hearing that. Maybe half-pint was right, and Jaycee had reached her limit.

Looking calm, Jaycee came into the kitchen and sat down beside Sam.

"I made coffee." Lizzie jumped up, grabbed mugs and the pot, then poured.

Sam didn't want to rush either of them, but he was anxious for information. "Everything check out okay?"

Jaycee nodded. "Thanks," she told Lizzie when she placed a mug before her.

Lizzie mouthed, "Just ask her." Then put his mug before him.

When she'd returned to her seat, Sam's patience cracked, and he followed Lizzie's advice. "Is this trouble about either of the prior incidents we've worked on?"

"No, it's not. Didn't I tell you that?" Surprised, Jaycee licked her lips and swiped at her face, clearly thinking back. "I'm sorry. I guess I didn't." She took a sip of her coffee, nearly spilled it, she was shaking so hard. "This is an entirely different incident."

Seizing the opening, Lizzie chimed in. "A witness incident that started on GDO."

Jaycee lifted her hand. "Better let me handle this part, Lizzie. You can go to your room for a while, if you like."

"She's protecting me," Lizzie told Sam. "But there's no need, Mom. Now that Sam's here, I'll just tell you. I witnessed what happened, too."

"At the park?" Jaycee's eyes widened and her mouth dropped

open. "No! You were in the restroom. I blocked the door with my foot."

"It's got a window." Lizzie lifted her arms. "I looked. I saw."

"You saw, and you didn't tell me right away?"

Lizzie shrugged then looked at Sam. "She was already freaked out. I didn't want to make it worse. I just wanted to get out of there."

Sam nodded but held his tongue.

Jaycee palmed her jaw. "I can't believe I didn't know this. I'm your mother, Lizzie. How could I not know this?" She narrowed her gaze on her daughter. "You should have told me. We could have talked about it."

"I didn't want to talk about it. It was scary, and you got more and more upset."

"Upset or not, I should have known. How can I explain things or comfort you, if I don't know—"

"I understood what happened just fine. Getting out of there was all the comfort I needed. I'm fine. Promise."

Sam watched them talk back and forth, trying to get a grip on exactly what had happened. But he failed. When they showed no signs of slowing down, he interrupted. "Whoa!" They fell silent, and he looked to Jaycee. "You get ready to start at the beginning." He swung his gaze to Lizzie. "What exactly is GDO?"

Lizzie retrieved the coffeepot and set it on the table. "We're isolated here, so now and then, we have an adventure."

"What kind of adventure?"

"A GDO—Girls Day Out." Lizzie frowned and spoke slowly. "Did you miss that?"

Jaycee placed her hand atop Lizzie's. "Let me."

Sam cranked his neck and stared at Jaycee, then again waited.

"Girls Day Out is an adventure where we do girl things," she explained. "We shop, have lunch, get our hair or nails done. You know, just girl stuff."

"Okay. I've got that." Sam drained his cup, reached for the pot, and refilled his mug. When he set it back down, he looked at Jaycee. "Now, start at the beginning. What happened?"

"We drove up to Scottsboro—"

"That's a haul," Sam said.

"A little over four hours," Jaycee said. "But we don't shop close to home."

"Ever?" What about buying milk or bread?

"Ever. Safety measure." She sipped from her own mug, then went on. "I bought a second laptop and Lizzie picked up a couple of tops. We shopped a while longer, and then had lunch at a lovely little restaurant."

"Their food is always great," Lizzie chimed in.

"Sounds like a nice enough day." Sam kept waiting for the shoe to fall. The park, the restroom, what Lizzie had seen out of that window. Suspecting it could take a while longer, now they were describing the food and the charming décor, he pulled up his reserve patience. They'd get there eventually, and he could pick up clues, letting them do it their way.

"It was a fabulous day." Jaycee dabbed at a spill spot near her sleeve with her napkin.

"Until we went to the park." Lizzie twisted her lips into a scrunch. "Shopping was almost fun. Well, it wasn't awful."

Half-pint still didn't like shopping. At least that hadn't changed. "What happened at the park?"

Lizzie's expression turned dark. "Things went south really fast."

"Jackson County Park would have been fine if it hadn't been so busy. But it was," Jaycee countered. "Crowds are way too risky." She dragged her thumb on the handle of her mug. "We didn't stop. Lizzie was pretty disappointed."

"Sure was. I needed to walk off the shopping stuff. Being stuck inside . . . I don't like it."

She never had. Sam hadn't either. His voice went deadpan. "I'm sure dessert after lunch had nothing to do with it, right?"

Lizzie eyed him suspiciously and sniffed. "Not likely. I had one little piece of chocolate cake."

"Let me guess. About a fourth of the whole cake." He cocked an eyebrow, knowing them too well to push. Jaycee had always handled stress this way. As if she talked about trouble aloud, it was real and unavoidable. So long as she didn't, she could manage it. She had to get to it in her own way, in her own time, and she would. Considering her history, he respected her process all the more. She didn't jump at shadows. She assessed, first striving for a clear mind and logic. "Seven layers?"

"Three layers, and probably a fourth of the whole cake." Lizzie looked down at the table.

"With double frosting," her mother piped in. "But who cares? Girls Day Out is supposed to be indulgent and fun."

"So, if you didn't stop at the park, how did things go south fast at the park?"

"We went to a different park," Jaycee said. "Lizzie was disappointed, and that's unacceptable on GDO, so I drove down toward Camden. There's a park near there that Lizzie loves."

"I used to love it," Lizzie corrected Jaycee, plucking a piece of lint from her cuff. "It has a cool gazebo and benches, great trails, a creek and it's never crowded." Lizzie's face sobered. "But I don't want to go back there again."

"Ever?" Sam asked.

"Never ever."

Strong reaction, and Lizzie didn't frighten easily. What had happened there?

CHAPTER FOUR

"We walked a bit and Lizzie had to use the restroom," Jaycee refilled her mug. Steam lifted off it, curled in the air. "There were only two other cars in the parking lot. One was a police cruiser and the other a black sedan. The cop stood in front of his cruiser, talking to two men—one had on a hoodie, the other a sweatshirt. I think they came together in the other car."

"Me, too, Sam."

He nodded but didn't dare to interrupt. It could take an hour to get back to this spot.

Jaycee shifted uneasily on her seat. "I didn't like the way Hoodie and Sweatshirt Guy were looking at us, so I kept my distance and sent Lizzie to the restroom. I made sure I could see the door from where I stood, which was close to it, and I pretended to be stone-deaf."

"Why?" Sam asked, hoping he didn't regret interrupting her.

"They were all arguing. I'm not sure what about. Hoodie had lost something that must have belonged to the cop, and Sweatshirt Guy insisted Hoodie stole it. The cop was playing referee, trying to sort it all out and get to the truth." Jaycee stiffened. "Things were heating up out there, and I got a really bad feeling. I ducked into the restroom to tell Lizzie to hurry then went back outside to keep my eye on them."

"Did they see you come back out?"

"No," Jaycee said. "They were too fired up by then." She fingered her collar. "The cop stepped away from them and turned his back to speak into his radio. It was up near his throat. Hoodie choked Sweatshirt Guy to death. I watched him go down."

Jaycee paused, sucked in breaths, hard and fast.

Sam covered her hand on the tabletop with his. Watching a man be murdered was enough to rattle anyone.

"The cop was yelling a blue streak, wanting to know what happened," Jaycee went on. "Hoodie told the cop all of a sudden Sweatshirt Guy just went down. He hadn't touched him."

"That's a lie, Sam." Lizzie narrowed her eyes. "I saw Hoodie choke him, just like Mom said."

Sam nodded, acknowledging her, then looked back to Jaycee.

She paled and continued, "I ducked into the restroom and told Lizzie we had to go now."

"I was all about that. Left with my hands sopping wet."

Jaycee nodded. "When I opened the door, the cop was standing just outside it. I pushed Lizzie back inside and propped my foot against the door to keep her in." Jaycee stiffened in her chair. "He said a man had a heart attack and died. An ambulance was on the way. I should go straight to my vehicle and not let my little girl see."

"What did you say?" Sam asked.

"Thank you for the warning, Officer."

"He had no idea either of you had seen the murder?"

"No." She drew in a stuttered breath. "He asked if I lived nearby. I told him, no. We were just passing through on our way from Atlanta."

Blinking hard, she paused a beat. "He asked my name, too. I gave him a fake one, Mary Ann Cook."

Sam rubbed at his beard. "Why did you do that?"

"Instinct."

"Wise, under the circumstances." Sam looked to Lizzie who nodded her agreement. "Then what?"

"I shielded Lizzie from the scene, and we left," Jaycee said. "I tried to block his vision of my tag, but he could have already gotten it."

Probably had. Sam lowered his hand to the table. "You ever see any of them before?"

"No."

"Me neither, Sam," Lizzie said, grabbing a tin of cookies and setting them open on the table. "Chocolate chip. Elle's recipe."

Nick's Elle made the best chocolate chip cookies. Sam snagged one. "The cop wasn't local, I take it."

"No." Jaycee paused a second, then dropped the napkin. "I ran online searches. The most similar uniform I've found was from a community called Shepard's Corner. It's just south of Selma. But it's not exact. Which makes me wonder if he was a real cop, or just posing as one. I found nothing on him." Jaycee lifted a cookie from the tin. "The victim, Sweatshirt Guy, was a Camden local named Judd Baker. Located him quickly. He was not a good guy. But no one deserves to be choked to death."

"What about Hoodie?" Sam asked.

"He's a cousin and partner-in-crime to Judd Baker."

"What kind of crimes?"

"Petty stuff, mostly, but drug charges, too."

The cop could have been fake. Come to the park expecting a shipment he then was to transport. In a sense, Sam was relieved. Seemed she got through this witnessing event unscathed. So, what had her freaked out? "Have you seen the cop or Hoodie since then?"

"No." From her tone, she didn't consider that good news. "But it appears one of them might have found me . . . maybe. Or someone else has. I'm not sure." She set her cookie on a fresh napkin and broke off a bite. "Which brings us to the current challenge and the reason I called you."

Witnessing a murder wasn't the current challenge? Sam tensed.

Lizzie hopped up and grabbed the coffeepot. "I'm thinking this is going to be a two-pot conversation." She brewed a second pot of coffee, filling the kitchen with the rich smells of cookies and fresh coffee, two of Sam's favorite scents.

Jaycee turned the topic. "Sam, I've been so rude. I'm sorry," she said. "How are the partners and Nora?"

"They're good and Nora is Nora. Still bossing everybody, and mothering every stray that comes around," he said. "She asks after you and Lizzie every time I see her."

The hint of a smile as haunted as her eyes lifted Jaycee's lips. "She would, bless her heart."

Lizzie returned to the table with the full fresh pot. "I'm going to have to jump in here because we can't make this briefing a three-pot discussion. My gut's slushing already." She patted her flat stomach and looked at Sam. "Mom's got a stalker. He's hanging Christmas stockings on the mailbox."

Jaycee frowned.

A stalker? Sam looked from Lizzie to Jaycee. "Tell me about this."

Jaycee refilled her mug. "About a week after our GDO, I walked up toward the road and spotted something red. It was a Christmas stocking hanging on the mailbox."

"It is pretty close to Christmas," Sam reminded her. "Could be a neighbor spreading Christmas cheer."

"It's not, Sam," Lizzie said. "GDO was November 20th. The stockings started Thanksgiving Day, November 26th."

"Started?" Sam frowned. "What do you mean started?"

"Just show him, Mom."

Jaycee left the table, disappeared down the hallway, then returned with a stack of eight Christmas stockings. "Inside each one of these is a note."

"I wrote the day and date on the back of each note," Lizzie said.

"Good thinking, half-pint."

"I think it could be the cop—if he is a cop," Jaycee said, passing the first stocking.

Sam examined it. Typical Christmas stocking available everywhere. He reached inside and pulled out the note. Calibri font, regular printer paper. Nothing remarkable. He then read the words.

"You lied, but I found you. You cannot hide, Jaycee." On the back, Lizzie had written in small print down in the corner, Thursday, November 26th. Thanksgiving Day.

Sam put the note back in the stocking. "I see why you think it could be the cop." She'd claimed she was Mary Anne Cook from Atlanta. He had gotten the tag and run it. "Do the others make you think it's him, too?"

"They don't," she said. "That's what makes this so scary."

Sam set the first stocking aside and wiggled his fingers for her to pass the second. "Give it back." Same font, same size, same paper. On the back: Thursday, December 10th.

He read the third through the seventh:

"I need it now, Jaycee. Just put it in the mailbox."

"Stop messing with me, Jaycee. I'm losing patience."

"Don't make me take what is mine."

"I know you're there. Do it, Jaycee."

"Don't disappoint me again. You and your little girl will regret it."

By the time he read the eighth note Sam was at war between fear and fury. "What happens now is on you. I warned you . . ."

He looked over at Jaycee. Her shaking hand was pressed against her mouth, and for the first time, he understood what half-pint had said about fear she'd break. It wasn't the threat against her. It was the threat against Lizzie. That's why Jaycee had called.

Her skin looked the color of paste. "Did you take something from the cop?" he asked her.

"Nothing."

"From anyone else?" Sam asked, truly puzzled.

"No, not a thing." Frustrated, Jaycee stood and paced. "I have no idea what I supposedly have that he wants back. If I knew, I'd give it to him. But we haven't been away from the cottage since GDO."

"Not at all?" That surprised him. "What about church?" They had gone every Sunday in Seagrove.

"We go online," Jaycee said.

"Groceries?"

She gestured no.

"That's been a month, Jaycee." Sam frowned at her.

"I know." She dropped back onto her seat and cast a sideward glance at the stockings. "Getting those all the time, we didn't dare venture out."

They'd been virtual prisoners here. Since before Thanksgiving. "We need a calendar."

"I did one." Lizzie disappeared for a second then returned with two sheets of paper. She'd printed one page for November, and a second one for December. Dates were circled in red. Message received that day penciled in. "What are these numbers?" He pointed to tiny digits at the bottom of the day's squares written in green. "6, 13, 16, 18, 20, 22, 23, 24."

"The number of days since GDO." Lizzie looked from the page to him. "The first stocking came six days after, the next thirteen, and so on." She hiked a shoulder. "I was looking for patterns."

"Clever." Sam nodded. He didn't see any patterns. The stalker left the stockings on different days of the week, at different times, and at different intervals between drops. "Did you find any?"

"No, I did not." Her disappointment was clear. "But the frequency sure has escalated. From nine days between the first two to every day for the last three."

"Good observation, half-pint." And the last stocking and note had been delivered this morning.

"Three days in a row," Lizzie said, her worry clear in her voice. "Whoever he is, he's coming for us, Sam."

It looked that way to Sam, too. "He does seem to be getting desperate." Escalating the intervals to daily drops and the tone of the messages themselves.

"That's my feeling on it, too," Jaycee said. "Desperate people do awful things. That's why I called you."

She'd called because she was scared to death. Whether these were from the park incident or one of the prior ones, someone was coming after them. Sam's insides curled. He looked from the pages over to her. Lizzie had put a hand on her mother's shoulder. He wished he could say something, anything, to ease their minds. But he wouldn't insult either of them with a platitude, and certainly not with a lie. "I take it you didn't call the local cops and get prints run on these notes."

"No," Jaycee answered. "I thought about it, but not knowing where the cop at the park works, if he was a real cop—"

"He looked like a real cop," Lizzie said. "He had the uniform, the cruiser and the radio, Mom."

"He did." Jaycee sighed. "I couldn't find him or his uniform, so I didn't call."

"I tested the notes for prints, Sam," Lizzie confessed. "Mom got me a kit for Christmas last year." Lizzie shrugged. "There were none."

"Not surprised, half-pint." She was good at this, and she'd tried to be as methodical and thorough as possible. A surge of pride in her seeped through him. "Good thinking."

"Sam," Jaycee reached over and clasped his arm. "Do you think these could have anything to do with NINA or the system development?"

"I don't think so," he said honestly, then relayed Warrington's status.

"I'm thinking he or his friends wouldn't be this patient," Lizzie said. "They'd just come in and get what they wanted whether we were here or not."

Sam agreed with her, but Jaycee looked a blink away from tears, so he kept the thought to himself.

"What about Costa Rica?" Jaycee frowned, her eyes piercing and haunted.

"I checked on that, too. Diego Vargas's replacement wants no part of any of us." At least that could relieve her mind on one front.

She let out a staggered sigh of relief. "That's one less, then."

Jaycee squeezed her eyes shut. When she didn't reopen them, Sam shot a questioning look at Lizzie. She shrugged.

"Jaycee?" He prodded her.

Finally, she opened her eyes and looked at him. "Sorry. I've been avoiding something because I'm afraid of the answer."

She didn't frighten any more easily than Lizzie, but he'd have to be a blind man not to see the fear in her now. "What answer are you afraid of?"

"The one to the question I haven't yet asked."

"What is it?" Sam softened his voice.

Her eyes stretched wide and tension pounded off of her in rolling waves. "Should we run?"

She feared uprooting their lives again. "Let's hold off on a decision on that for the time being," Sam said. "We'll put up some surveillance cameras and see if they tell us anything about this stalker first."

"Mom already tried that," Lizzie told Sam. "Game cameras."

"It's a sedan," Jaycee said. "I can't tell the color—black-and-white—but the car is either black or deep blue . . .something dark like that. Baker's cousin, Hoodie, drives a green truck."

"What color was the sedan at the park?"

"Black," Lizzie said. "Rear right fender was dented. The one we caught on the game camera isn't."

Could have fixed it. "Anything on the driver?" Sam asked.

Lizzie nodded no. "Windows are tinted really dark." She pulled out her phone and began pressing buttons. "I've got pics but can't tell if it's a man or woman. All I see is a gender-neutral coat sleeve and a black glove." She flipped the phone for Sam to look.

He nearly smiled. Half-pint had always been observant and interested in investigation skills. He'd taught her a lot, and she'd learned even more. He cycled through the photos. "No tag shot?"

"No tag," she said. "Or else it was covered in mud." She swiped to that photo on her phone, then passed it back to Sam.

Sam couldn't see a license plate at all. "You did great, Lizzie."

She smiled. "Really?"

"Seriously good." He didn't smile. But he had to work at it. "Proud of you."

"Thanks, Sam."

He winked.

CHAPTER FIVE

4:47 PM

Just after dark, Sam walked down the trail to the road and stopped to examine the ground near the mailbox. There were ruts but it had rained so getting a decent tire-track cast was out of the question. He lit the area with a flashlight and snapped a few photos anyway, then called the office.

"PSC."

Recognizing Tim's voice, Sam said, "Hey, buddy. I need a delivery." He relayed the address Lizzie had given him, the shell lot near the pond. "The only place to land a chopper is a shell lot."

"We'll handle it. Grabbing a pen." A beat later, Tim added, "Okay, shoot."

"Four outdoor surveillance cameras. At least two of them need audio capability. I need a rifle and scope, a backup Glock, and a residential security system that ties directly to my phone."

"To police too, right?"

"No. No police."

"Oh, boy."

"Yeah." Sam parked a hand at his hip.

"What about backup?"

"No, no backup at this time. It's best I handle this myself."

"What's going on, Sam?" Worry laced Tim's voice. "They okay?"

"So far, but someone is knocking at their door."

"Anyone we know?"

"Not sure, yet." Sam looked up and then down the road. "My gut says no, this is a different incident."

"Oh, no," Tim said. "She witnessed something else?"

"A murder. Her and Lizzie." Admitting that had Sam's throat burning. "But it isn't for fact that's the issue."

"There's more?"

"My girls have a Christmas Stocking stalker."

"You're serious?" Tim's surprise mirrored Sam's own.

"He wants something he thinks they have, but they don't have any idea what he's talking about." Sam relayed the notes, the specifics on them.

"They just can't catch a break." Tim's disgust rippled through his voice and the phone.

Sam felt it in every cell in his body. "Not with both hands and a net."

"Sam, I really think we should come and help you."

It was just a few days until Christmas. He didn't want to pull them away from their families. "Not yet. This is about Jaycee and Lizzie. If I run into something I can't handle, I'll be first to call."

"You know, this doesn't make a lot of sense." Tim cleared his throat. "If she doesn't know who he is or where he's from, what can she tell authorities? Nothing."

"Could be someone else," Sam said. "I just don't know yet."

"How many persons of interest are there?"

"Three," Sam said on a heartfelt sigh. "So far."

"I'll gather up your gear and some additional tools you might find handy and give you a call to coordinate the pickup."

"Thanks, Tim."

Sam disconnected the call and walked back toward the cabin. The night was cold, the air brisk, and the wind rustling through the trees was about the only sound around. It was pitch dark. No lights from neighbors—there were none—or town. In the far distance, the sky brightened a little, but otherwise it was woods, stars and a sickle moon. Peaceful place, but too remote for Jaycee and Lizzie on their own. Half-pint could drive, but she wouldn't be legal to do it until after her birthday. What if Jaycee couldn't drive? Lizzie would do it anyway. He knew that, but he hated that she'd have to do that, too. This kind of life was no life for them. They deserved so much better. So much more.

He made a pass around the cabin. Jaycee stood in the kitchen preparing a meal. He walked past the living room window, noted the gap at the lock was a little wide. He walked on, toward the kitchen window, studying the ground by flashlight. No footprints or anything unusual. He swung the beam and homed in on the lock. Narrower gap than at the living room. "Now, now," he mumbled to himself. "What is this about?"

A pot clanged. He looked up and saw a startled Jaycee staring at him gape-jawed, her hand at her chest.

"It's me, Sam!" He raised his voice.

Even muffled by the glass, she heard him, grasped the ledge of the sink and bowed her head.

Double-timing it, he hit the porch and opened the door. "I'm so sorry, Jaycee. I didn't mean to startle you."

"It's okay." She blew out a long breath. "It's fine. Fine."

When that woman said fine, it was never fine. He walked over to her, turned her into his arms and just held her close. "You're all right. Everything is all right."

She let out a little moan and pulled herself taller. "I guess I'm a little jumpy."

Lizzie came in, smelling of soap. She'd been in the shower. "What's going on?"

"Just fixing dinner." Jaycee faked a smile.

Lizzie looked at Sam. "I was outside looking around and startled your mother. Totally my fault."

"It's no big deal." Jaycee stepped away and recovered the pot full of potatoes. "Shoo! I need to mash these while they're hot."

Lizzie seemed to relax then, and Sam walked over to the living room window. Checked out that gap. He motioned to Lizzie to come to him. "Locks busted," he said. "You know anything about that?"

"No." She looked up at Sam. "Mom checked when we came in."

She had. And if she'd seen anything, she would have mentioned it. "Maybe she didn't notice," Sam told Lizzie. "It looks fine, but the gap is wide."

"There's a strip of something there, between the lock and the window."

Sam took a closer look. "Indeed, there is."

"What is it?" Lizzie said, bobbing in for a better look.

"It's a magnetic strip that keeps the signal intact on an alarm system while you open the window."

"It bypasses the system and the alarm won't go off."

"That's right."

"Um, Sam. We don't have an alarm system." She lifted a shoulder. "Out here, who would need one?"

"But if you want in and you don't know there isn't an alarm, this is what you do."

"She is going to totally freak that someone got in our house without her knowing it." Lizzie blinked hard and fast. "We've liked it here but she's going to run. We're going to move again."

"Quit borrowing trouble. Enough finds us on its own."

"You don't get it. She won't stay here, Sam. There are no second chances. She's too scared for me."

"Help me check the other windows and let's see exactly what we're looking at."

He went one way, she the other. Minutes later, they met back in the hallway. "You find anything, half-pint?"

"Nothing."

"Say nothing about this," Sam said. "It might have been this way since you guys moved here. Maybe that's why she didn't say anything about it."

"But it isn't safe, Sam. We can't live in a cabin that isn't safe."

He frowned. "Would I let you live somewhere not safe?"

"I don't think so."

"I wouldn't." He gripped her shoulders gently. "I've got gear inbound. We'll have this resolved in no time."

"There you two are." Jaycee smiled. "Dinner's ready."

"I could have helped you, Jaycee." Sam walked to the table.

"Thanks, but no thanks." She shot him an apologetic look. "I've eaten your cooking."

"It's not that bad."

"True." Lizzie grunted. "But it ain't this good, either. Mom took lessons from Betsy."

His housekeeper and cook. "Forgot that. Well, you've got me there."

Jaycee and Lizzie took their seats. Sam joined them, sat and folded his hands. "Lizzie, you do the honors."

She offered up a prayer and ended with, "Thanks for sending Sam to help us—again. Amen."

"Amen." Sam smiled. The kid had stolen his heart years ago and she still held it. She always would.

"Chess after dinner?" she challenged Sam.

"When I get back." He noticed his Yeti was on the table and full of fresh iced tea. "Thanks, Jaycee."

She nodded. "I noticed you still have a glass with you most of the time."

"Yes, I do."

She spooned mashed potatoes onto her plate. "I also noticed not so much as a whiff of jalapeño juice. Have you lost your preference for it?"

He laughed. "I have."

She and Lizzie laughed with him. "I'm sure Nora is really happy about that."

"So she says."

"Wait. You said when you get back." Jaycee stopped, her fork mid-air. "You're leaving?"

"He's going to get some gear he needs." Lizzie looked at him. "He won't be long. Right, Sam?"

"An hour. Maybe a few minutes longer. That's all." Jaycee's reaction confused him. She'd been living out here for two years and she looked close to panic about him leaving?

She hadn't been living out here with a stalker after her.

"An hour." She calmed down, and relief settled in.

"An hour isn't long," Lizzie said, reassuring herself as much as her mother.

His heart thumped and his stomach burned. The food going into his mouth that had been so good had grown tasteless. How many times in the past six years had they been this afraid?

He looked from one to the other. Sharing uneasy, wary looks, he knew the answer. And it had resentment in him rising.

Way too many.

CHAPTER SIX

8:47 PM

Sam retrieved the supplies Mark himself had flown in, spent a few minutes giving him a rundown on events and filled him in on the park incident. He would take the Baker cousin and the purported cop from there.

On the way back to the cabin at the bend on the winding road, he phoned Jaycee to put her and Lizzie's minds at ease. "It's me. Just letting you know I'm back."

"I don't see your truck," Jaycee said.

"I'm at the mailbox. I want to take care of a little business before coming in. Won't be long."

"Need any help?"

He'd love to be with her, but she was safer in the cabin. "Lizzie will feel vulnerable," he said. "Best stay with her."

"Agreed. She's extra jumpy."

So was Jaycee. And so was he. The escalation in the threats gave them all just cause for elevated concern. "See you in a few minutes."

He worked quickly, installing cameras at the mailbox in nearby trees, then one on the roadside of the cabin and on each side. Finally, he went inside.

The relief on Jaycee's face was palpable. "I made you fresh tea."

Her smile trembled. He took the glass, drank a long swallow. "Thanks. I was thirsty."

Lizzie came in wearing pink-and-green PJs that covered everything but her neck, head and fingertips. "You cold, half-pint?"

"Not anymore." She walked over to the chessboard. "We're good to go."

A small Christmas tree had been placed in the corner near the front window. It wasn't yet decorated. "Would you rather decorate the tree?"

"Christmas Eve." She sat down and motioned to him. "Come on, let's play."

Jaycee sat down on the end of the sofa closest to them to watch. Sam hung his coat and hat on the rack, then made his way to the chessboard. He sat down and rubbed his hands together. "You go first."

The game was on. And Lizzie surprised him. "Are you a ringer?"

She laughed. He loved the sound.

"I've been playing against myself."

"Not against your mother?" He cast a glance at Jaycee.

"She passed me up a long time ago."

Jaycee was no slouch. "Where did you learn all these moves?"

"Online," Lizzie said. "The master's games are all posted. I studied them."

"Mmm," Sam mumbled. "Looks like you've passed me up, too."

"She's holding back, Sam." Jaycee nodded, adding weight to her claim.

"Is she now?" He sent Lizzie a narrow-eyed look. "Is that a fact?"

Her cheeks flushed red. "Maybe just a little bit."

He took her bishop.

"Whoa!" Lizzie's jaw dropped. "Nice move, Sam."

"Thanks."

She took his queen and laughed deeply.

Sam stroked his beard. "Didn't see that one coming."

Jaycee's tinkle of laughter joined Lizzie's. The sounds warmed Sam's heart. "I'm definitely going to have to brush up." He smiled at Lizzie. "Well done."

"On that happy note," Lizzie stood up, "I'm going to bed. You guys probably want to talk anyway."

Sam did. "Night, half-pint."

She walked over and hugged him. "You just have to ask her. That's all."

"Okay." He supposed she was right. With Jaycee, she never burdened anyone else with anything. But if you asked, she'd give you honest answers. "Sweet dreams."

Lizzie squeezed him harder. "Love you." She backed up, then quickly disappeared down the hallway.

Sam couldn't speak, couldn't move for a long minute. His heart had melted. Why of all the partners Lizzie had chosen him, Sam had no idea. But she had, and he loved her for it. She'd wormed her way into every chamber of his heart and would always remain there.

"You're humbled," Jaycee said.

No sense denying it. "Someone loving you who isn't obligated to is a humbling thing."

"It is." Jaycee's eyes looked glossy. "Lizzie lets so few people into her world. I'm glad she has you, Sam. I worry about that with her."

"She's discerning not anti-social. Trust has to be as hard for her as for you, considering what you two have been through—are going through."

"We thank God for you every day," Jaycee said. "Just knowing if we call, you'll be on the other end of that line . . ." Her voice softened. "It makes a lot of difference to us."

Lizzie's saying to her mother she could handle this in three words came back to Sam. There'd been no reservation or uncertainty in her. She'd known if she uttered their code-word, he would act. "So long as I'm breathing, Jaycee. Promise."

She sniffed. "I'm so sorry I ruined your Christmas plans."

He went over and sat down beside her, put his tea on the table in front of them next to hers. "You didn't."

"I know I did," she said. "Your brother and sister always come home for Christmas."

"That was when the folks were there. Now that they've passed, it's hit or miss. This year, it's a total miss. I'd be on my own."

"Why?"

"They have families and kids with Christmas programs at church, school events and friends. They don't want to miss everything at home to come to Summerland."

"It's an ordeal for them to coordinate their lives, I'm sure."

He nodded. "They're building their own traditions and memories. Can't fault them for that. Their kids need it."

"True," she agreed. "But what about the partners?"

"They're all married now, doing their own family things." He went on to catch her up on everyone's lives, and those in Seagrove Village she and Lizzie had been closest to while there.

"Life does go on, doesn't it?" Jaycee looked wistful. "But I'm sure every one of the partners invited you over for Christmas dinner."

"They did."

"But you didn't want to intrude."

She'd pegged him exactly. "Christmas is for family."

"I'd remind you that those guys are your extended family, but I'm in no position to lecture. I struggle with the same challenge about my parents. I wonder often if they're still alive, and how they're doing. It kills me to not be able to contact them, especially on Christmas."

He made a mental note of that. To check on them and see how things were there. "I'm sure it does."

"I'm sorry about your mom, Sam." Jaycee placed a hand on his arm. "She was a wonderful woman."

He nodded.

"When did it happen?"

"Two years ago, come Valentine's Day." He blinked hard. "Cancer." He tilted his head. "I knew it was coming soon. She told me the day before that she missed my dad." He looked at Jaycee. "She missed him every day since we buried him, but that was the only time she ever said the words out loud. I knew she was ready."

"While we're poorer for her passing, Heaven is richer." Jaycee squeezed his arm.

"We are, and it is."

"So, you really would have been alone on Christmas." A frown settled in between her brows that wrinkled her skin. "I'm doubly glad then that you are here with us. You should not be alone on Christmas."

Telling, that remark. Four days until Christmas and she expected him to still be here. "You're alone every year. Well, you and Lizzie."

"No choice." She shrugged.

They'd had wonderful Christmas celebrations when in Seagrove Village. What a miserable twist of fate they'd had to leave. Lizzie and Jaycee had thrived there. Now, here, they were isolated and alone. "I take it you're homeschooling, Lizzie."

Jaycee nodded, tucked her knees up under her. "She loves it. You know how she hates being confined."

"She must miss having friends, especially at her age."

"If she does, she doesn't talk about it. I have to say, I worry about it, but she insists she's fine."

He hoped she meant it and not what Jaycee meant when she said she was fine. She was anything but fine. "While I was out, I spoke with your point of contact." The witness protection assigned one she could phone if she got into trouble and needed immediate assistance.

"He says there's been no activity on your case in nearly two years—including word from you."

She flushed. "We like it here. We wanted to plant some roots, so I didn't let anyone know where we were, including him."

"And you put additional safety measures into place."

She nodded. "We wanted to stay."

"I understand that, but you still need someone you can rely on in a pinch."

"We have someone," she told him. "Three words and you were on your way."

"Your contact wanted me to pass along some information to you."

Worry flashed in her eyes. "Tell me Warrington is still in jail."

Sam nodded. "Maximum security in Colorado."

"They moved him? I saw nothing of that on the net."

"Three months ago. He killed two other inmates and a prison guard."

"If he ever gets out . . ."

"He won't."

Her eyes darted. "Then this stalking incident can't be about that."

"I don't think it is. Or about Costa Rica." Sam stroked his beard. "Trouble is, the park incident doesn't feel quite right for it."

"It doesn't to me, either." Clearly, that scared her most of all.

"I'm guessing the purported cop got your information from running your tag through DMV."

"That wouldn't help him much, but I guess it's possible. This address isn't on my tag or my driver's license."

"What address is?"

"One in Scottsboro." She licked at her lips. "We pick up mail on trips there."

She hadn't been there since the park incident. "So, if not through DMV, how do you think this stalker found you?"

"I have no idea, which is why it has me terrified." She swallowed hard. "Well, that and not knowing what he wants."

"You witnessed a murder."

"But he doesn't know that."

"He might, Jaycee."

"Logic gap," she said. "If he thought for a second that I had seen the murder, he would never have let us leave that park." She started shaking again. "He never would have waited six days to start stalking us."

"Maybe it took him that long to find you."

He wants something back," she reminded Sam. "A witness can't un-see something seen, and there's nothing to give back." Jaycee sank her teeth into her lower lip. "He is after something tangible. I have no idea what, but something tangible."

"The notes agree." Sam watched her. "But to give back, you must first take."

"I took nothing," Jaycee insisted. "Nothing."

"I know." Sam swallowed a sip of tea, returned his glass to the table. Jaycee tensed even more, shook harder, looking brittle and so fatigued. She'd been on edge since he'd arrived. Tonight at dinner, she'd pushed her food around on her plate but only had eaten three bites. The dark circles under her eyes had become even more pronounced, the haunted look in them bolder. He hated that haunted look. Hated those circles. Hated her not eating, and he really hated her shaking and scared. Every one of those things tore at his heart. Now, she looked a blink from tears. He hated that most of all.

She held her silence, staring off far beyond the walls of the cabin.

"Jaycee?"

A long moment later, she looked over at him. Turbulence in her pounded out with the force of hammer blows. "Why do these things keep happening to me, Sam?" She lifted a frustrated hand. "I'm just trying to do what's right and raise my daughter and live a quiet life. That's all. Now this witness thing is happening to Lizzie, too. Just a quiet life. A little peace. Is that asking for too much?"

He had no answers, and he refused to insult her by pretending that he did. When the first tear fell and glistened on her cheek, he lifted his outstretched arms. "It's asking for very little. Come here."

She turned to him and he closed his arms around her, his chest tight. He whispered a prayer for her, for Lizzie, feeling Jaycee's silent tears soak his shirt. He had no answers. She knew as well as he that there were no answers. "God works in mysterious ways, honey. He specializes in making ways where there are none."

"I know. I'm just . . .so tired of this battle, Sam. I am so tired of it."

Her whole body shivered with silent sobs. His eyes burned and his throat went tight. Necessity demanded she be fiercely independent for herself and Lizzie, and never had he met a stronger or braver woman. She'd stood up against a team of dirty bureaucrats and the darkest forces of evil in human form on the planet, ones who had hunted her, and while he'd been able to assist in her extractions, she'd had to cope with the daily torture of wondering if every day would be the day they would find her and Lizzie. If that would be the day they would die. He did all he could, but he couldn't take any of that worry and justifiable fear off her shoulders.

Yet, there was one thing he could do for her. The one thing after prayer that everyone needed when confronted and confounded by crisis and regretting the choices they had made that led to irrevocable and unavoidable challenges, second-guessing themselves on whether or not what they had done had been right. He could hold her while she cried.

So he did, and inwardly he wept with her.

CHAPTER SEVEN

Arlington, Alabama
Tuesday, December 22, 1:30 AM

Sam's phone dinged.

The priority tone awakened him, and he gently unwound his arms from Jaycee. She'd fallen asleep sitting on the sofa, and he hadn't had the heart to wake her and send her to bed. She'd been so upset and needed the rest as much as she'd needed a good cry.

Stepping into the kitchen, he opened the monitoring app. The mailbox out by the road filled his phone screen. A gray Volvo pulled up to it and stopped. When the window lowered, Sam clicked to snap capture a photo. Male driver. Mid-thirties. Ordinary looking. No distinguishing features. He hung the Christmas stocking on the mailbox and then sped away. Sam clicked several more times, trying to capture the tag, but something—he took a closer look—a sheet of paper taped over the tag with silver duct tape blocked the view. It wasn't high-tech, but the paper and tape were effective.

Sam fired off photos of it, the vehicle and driver with a note to the office, asking them to check out the person for an ID and the vehicle for an owner. Maybe they'd get lucky and get a match. If anyone could find either, it'd be Nick. Under his hand, computers sang.

Jaycee stirred, rubbing her eyes. They were tear-swollen and red. "Sam, what's going on?"

"Another stocking has been delivered." He showed her a photo of the man. "You recognize him?"

Jaycee studied the image hard. "There's a niggle of something familiar about him, but I can't slot from where or why."

"So, he's no one you really know, then?"

"No. But maybe Lizzie will recognize him. She's got a mind like a steel trap."

She did. Sam stowed the phone. "We'll ask her when she wakes up." He swiped to a photo of the vehicle. "Do you recognize this car?"

"No." Jaycee smiled. "At least now I know what he looks like. I can see him coming."

That confused Sam.

She picked up on it. "That's not why I'm smiling."

"Okay." Now he was totally lost. And puzzled.

She picked up on that, too. "Thank you for holding me. I really needed to be held."

It was time to talk straight. He'd called himself forty kinds of fool for the past six years. "If I hadn't thought I'd get you and Lizzie killed, I'd have asked you to marry me six years ago. I want you to know the only reason I didn't was because I knew you had to leave to stay safe."

"I thought so, too. Everyone did. My point of contact, the guys at PSC, Nora."

"Nora knew you were in witness protection?"

Jaycee nodded. "I didn't tell her. I thought Lizzie had, but Nora insisted she had figured it out on her own."

"I had no idea." Sam grunted. "So why does she always ask me how you're doing?"

"I wondered that, too. But this is Nora, Sam. Who knows what all goes on in her mind?"

"She was checking to see if you were still on my mind," he guessed. "Not letting me forget, even knowing that would never happen." He looked at Jaycee. "You left, and I let you to keep you safe. But you haven't felt safe, have you?" Neither safe, nor content.

"There have been moments of grace." She looked up at him. "Really. But . . ."

"But what?"

"Fate keeps intervening, demanding more and more." She padded across the floor to the kitchen and got a glass of water, then took a long sip. "Hard truths hammer me a lot, and that, as you say, is a fact."

He sat down at the table with his glass of tea. "What kind of hard truths?"

"Guilt mostly." She took a seat near him. "I chose to be a whistleblower, but Lizzie didn't. Yet, she's living with my choices, and it's not fair." Jaycee swept a hand through her hair, shoved it back from her face. "Her life is no life for her, Sam. She has no friends, no school, no social life, nothing."

"She has you."

"Lucky her. She has a mother who falls into one crisis after another." Jaycee parked her chin on her hand, bent elbow atop the table. "I often wonder if she'd have been better off if she'd stayed in Seagrove Village with Kelly and Ben."

They were good friends to them both and the wealthy philanthropists and owners of Crossroads Crisis Center. In the event something happened to Jaycee, they were to have been Lizzie's guardians.

"Lizzie wouldn't be content without you," Sam said. "When you ran to avoid NINA and left Lizzie with Ben and Kelly at the Crisis Center, that was a hard time for Lizzie. She was beside herself. All she could think or talk about was getting you back home."

"She would have adapted. Ben and Kelly promised she would have a home with them. Be part of their family."

"You are her family. It would have been good, but not the same." Sam placed a hand on her arm. "She loves you, Jaycee."

"And I love her. Which is why I hate what our lives have become. I want more for her, Sam. I want more for me, too."

"What more do you want?" he asked.

"Something." She looked away then lifted a hand. "More than this." She let out a sigh. "I want a life. A family and a home. That's all I ever wanted. I have my work—"

"What work?"

"I do remote accounting for firms online." She sighed again. "I like a simple life. But not a nearly empty life."

Sam studied his hand on the table. "If I had asked you to marry me, what would you have said?"

"I'd have asked if you love me. I know you love Lizzie as if she's your own daughter."

"Saying goodbye and not being free to get in touch . . .nearly killed me."

"It did her, too."

Not *us*. *Her*. Intentional or deliberate? "But I'm not talking about Lizzie right now. I'm talking about you." He pushed harder. "If I had told you I love you and asked you to marry me, what would you have said?"

"If I knew it wouldn't get you killed?"

He nodded.

"I'd have said yes." She bent closer and pressed a gentle kiss to his lips. "But you didn't ask, and that time has gone."

"I was trying to do the right thing for you and Lizzie."

"Aren't we all?" She gave him a sad smile, touched a hand to his shoulder, then walked out of the room and down the hallway. A few minutes later, he heard the shower.

"You could ask her again now, Sam."

He whipped around toward the voice. "Lizzie! What are you doing up? It's the middle of the night."

"Eavesdropping." She said it without a hint of apology.

"Bad form, that." He took a drink of tea. It felt cool sliding down his throat.

52

"I need to know what is going on. I don't want you two messing it all up again." Lizzie walked closer, took the seat her mother had vacated. "We love you, Sam. We never should have left you. Mom cried a whole week, non-stop."

"A week's not that long, half-pint."

"It is for her."

She had him there. "It's complicated."

"What's so complicated?" Lizzie raised her hands then moved one up, one down, like shifting weights on scales. "Bad guys are after her. Bad guys are always after you. You love her. She loves you. You both love me." She dropped her leveled arms. "Nothing complicated about it. It's simple." Lizzie stood up. "The problem is you both think too much. Life ain't ever perfect, Sam. We take what we get and make the best of whatever we've got. No matter what that is, it's love that makes life beautiful."

"Nora?" he asked.

"Lizzie."

"Wise."

She hugged him, pleased by his praise. "Think about marrying mom."

"I will. But don't get set on it. She might say no."

"Never know, I guess, unless you ask." Lizzie looked a little smug. "I have a question."

"What's that?"

"You still collect all that old stuff?"

His 1800s memorabilia collection was one of the best in the world. "I do, though I don't keep much of it at Summerland anymore."

Her face echoed her disappointment. "I love that junk. Why isn't it at Summerland?"

"Some people who love that junk as much as we do came to see me. They wanted to take it with them."

"You sold it?" Horror screeched across her face.

He smiled at her outrage. "Course not. It's in Birmingham in a museum."

"A museum. Wow. I guess that's okay, then. I'd love to see it."

"They did it right, half-pint. It's something to behold."

Glass shattered.

Sam shot to his feet. "Go to your mother. Hurry, Lizzie. Get down and stay down until I come get you."

She flew down the hallway.

Sam retrieved his gun and checked the window with the busted lock. The windowpane remained intact. He'd definitely heard glass shatter. He scanned and a bright orange glow caught his eye.

Jaycee's SUV was on fire. The windshield had a gaping hole in it.

The notification came through. Sam hit the app on his phone . . . and caught a glimpse of a black sedan spinning out onto the road, heading south.

Ordinarily, he'd be out the door, chasing it down. But he didn't dare leave Jaycee and Lizzie stranded here. The fire could be a setup to flush him out. Could be more than one person; could have an army out there. He lifted his phone to call the police, order a BOLO to look out for the sedan. At three in the morning, traffic couldn't be that busy.

His finger on the dial, Sam hesitated. One of the men at the park had been a cop . . . maybe. Sam stowed his phone. He couldn't risk it.

"Sam?" A wide-eyed Jaycee appeared at the mouth of the hallway, her Glock in her hand. The same one he'd taught her to shoot. "What happened?"

"We're fine." He checked the clearing where her vehicle still burned. "But I'm afraid your SUV is toast."

She walked over to him and looked out the window to the blaze. "Thank goodness it wasn't parked any closer to your truck. It would have blistered the paint."

Smoke billowed up into the pre-dawn sky. "But it didn't."

She looked over at him. "Did you see anyone?"

"No, but I saw the car. Black sedan."

"Let me see." She wiggled her fingers at his phone.

He scrolled to the photo. "Is it the same one you saw at the park? Anyone else you might know?"

"No, I don't know anyone, but I don't think this is the same car from the park."

"Are you sure?"

"Lizzie said it had a dent in the back fender," Jaycee reminded him. "This one doesn't."

She stepped closer and looked closely at him. "You're not hurt, right? Please, tell me you're not hurt."

"I'm fine." He was ticked to the gills. Worried to death about ever leaving her and Lizzie alone again. "Just fine." He dragged a thumb over her jawline. "You keep an eye on Lizzie. I'm going to put the fire out and take a look around." He grabbed his coat and hat from the hook. "Lock the door, and don't open it until I return."

She nodded, worry flooding her eyes.

Outside, Sam listened for any sounds that didn't belong. But beyond the crackle of the fire, he noted none. Scanning the woods, he saw no movement, no signs of anyone waiting to ambush. Still, he followed protocol and cleared the area.

On video, the car had swept in, the driver tossed what appeared to be a Molotov cocktail type of incendiary device through Jaycee's windshield, then sped away. Sam's recon found nothing to suggest that others also had been there. The sedan driver had been flying solo. At least, that was good news.

He walked over and ran a check on his truck. Under the back bumper, his hand glided over a foreign object. He pulled out a flashlight and took a look. A tracking device.

Apparently, someone else had been out here. Long enough to plant the tracker on his bumper. Question was, did that and her SUV happen in one event, or in two?

He called the office, and when Nick answered, Sam said, "Great. Exactly who I needed to talk to."

"Before dawn?"

"Afraid so." Sam toed the dirt, spotted footprints near the tree line, beyond the clearing where the vehicles were parked. "Not my call."

"Whose was it?"

"I'm hoping you can tell me the answer to that." He filled Nick in on Jaycee's car and then on the device found under his bumper.

"Is there a number on it?"

"Lemme look." Sam scanned it with the light and spotted it. "There is," he said to Nick, then reeled off the number.

"I'm going to have to call a friend on this. I can get the information, but I'll trigger alarms we don't want triggered. He won't trigger anything."

Sam knew exactly who Nick was going to bring into the loop. Omega One at Home Base Command. He was PSC's point of contact and completely trusted. "Sounds great to me."

"Since you're not bellowing, I'm assuming Lizzie and Jaycee are okay."

"Yeah, they're okay." This wouldn't do a thing to lessen their worry. Jaycee was spiked off the charts already. "Rattled, but okay."

"You know, Sam, far be it from me to tell you your business, but it'd be a lot easier to protect them if they were here."

Sam snarled. "You been talking to Joe?"

"Yeah, of course," Nick said without seeming to take offense. "To be honest, we've all been talking. You know we're invested in you and in them, too."

The guys were and always had been. Nick had been great to Lizzie when NINA interdicted Jaycee in the village, and she'd been stashed for safekeeping. Ben and Kelly hadn't brought Sam and the team into the need-to-know loop and they'd feared Jaycee had disappeared for good. Lizzie had been so scared, and Nick had helped her though it. That took the temper right out of Sam. Of course, they were all worried, too. Crossing his chest with an arm, Sam stared off into the trees. "So, what exactly did you guys conclude?"

"Depends on whether or not you still love her, and she still loves you. If so, bring her home and marry her. Bring Lizzie, too, of course."

"Uh-huh." Sam stroked his beard. "And does she get a vote in this?"

"Lizzie?"

"Her, too, but I meant Jaycee."

"Yeah. I said if she loves you. You really do need to work on your listening skills, Sam."

"I appreciate you guys being concerned, buddy, but you'd best let me handle my personal life."

"None of us would consider interfering. We trust your judgment enough to put our lives in your hands routinely. That said, you asked, so I told you the truth. Friends do that."

They did, so Sam held his silence.

"I will say this, friend-to-friend." Nick paused, clearly determined to phrase this just right. "Either way, what you need is a plan."

Sam grunted. "Well, it so happens I agree with you on that, and I've been working on one." A flash of light in the house caught his attention. Jaycee in her bedroom, peeking out from a gap in the drapes. "Give me a yell when you get the traceback on that tracker."

"Wait," Nick protested. "Aren't you going to tell me your plan?"

"Nah, I don't guess I am." Small satisfaction, but Sam would take what he could get.

"Run it by Lizzie, then."

Sam halted his turn back to the cabin. "What?"

"Run your plan by Lizzie," Nick said. "She's sharp, and it's her life, too."

He had a point. She'd had little say in too much of it so far. "I'll handle it, Nick."

The smoke was dissipating and the sun teasing the sky with pale pink and gold streaks when Sam returned to the porch. He knocked the dirt off his boots and raised his hand to knock on the door.

Jaycee opened it just before his fist connected, nearly getting herself a face full of knuckles.

She ducked. "Sorry."

Mortified, Sam was glad she had fast reflexes. "That was close."

"I heard you on the porch." She sniffed. "Burned SUV is not a pleasing scent." Worry filled her eyes. "Your new truck is okay, right?"

"It's fine, but I'm afraid your SUV is totaled." He stepped

inside. "Everything else out there looks okay." No sense mentioning the tracker until he heard back from Nick.

"Coffee is ready." She started toward the kitchen.

"Great." He watched her round the corner of the island bar. "Is Lizzie up?"

"She's up." Lizzie came stumbling into the kitchen, her hair sleep-tossed, her eyes wide. "What's going on?"

"Sam's truck is okay, but someone set fire to our SUV," Jaycee said, reaching for mugs. "You want coffee?"

Lizzie nodded, accepting the news about the vehicle in stride.

She was still low drama.

"Did you report it?" Lizzie asked Sam.

Jaycee stopped cold, awaited his answer.

"Not to the police. Nick's taking a look."

Noting their relief, Sam removed his coat and hung it and his hat on the hook, then met them at the kitchen table. "Since we're all up, let's take a pause and review events one more time."

CHAPTER EIGHT

December 22, 5:30 AM

"Two sips first, then we start."

Sam nodded at Lizzie. A two-sip request was fair. He wanted her clear-headed for the review.

Jaycee kept watching the door, as if she expected someone to burst through it. Sam assured her the property was clear. No one was around. When she nodded and some of the tension in her eased, Sam retrieved a notebook, then turned to a fresh page.

"I'm ready," Lizzie said, no longer leaning her head on her hand. "Where do you want to start?"

Sam noted the date and time. "GDO."

Jaycee opened her mouth, but Lizzie held up a hand. "Sorry, Mom. I'm not awake enough to take the scenic tour. May I?"

Biting a half-smile from her lips, Jaycee nodded.

Sam sent Lizzie a look of gratitude she pretended not to see.

"We drove up to Scottsboro in Jackson County, went shopping—which wasn't totally awful—then had lunch, which was great. Afterward, we went to Jackson County Park, but it was too busy, so we didn't stop. Mom drove down to the park near Camden. The incident happened and we came home. That's pretty much it for GDO."

Sam opened his phone and cycled to the photo he and Jaycee wanted Lizzie with the steel-trap mind to view. "Do you know this man?"

"I don't know him."

"Does he look at all familiar?" Sam asked, recalling he had to Jaycee, though she couldn't peg why.

"I haven't seen that photo," Lizzie said, "But I have seen the man."

Jayce gasped. "Where, Lizzie?"

She swung her gaze from Sam to her mother. "At Unclaimed Baggage. He was in the store." Lizzie narrowed her eyes. "Don't you remember, Mom? It was when that baby was crying so loud."

"You're right. I remember now. He was fussing with the sales-clerk about something, but I couldn't hear him over the crying baby."

"He wanted the laptop you just bought from the other sales-clerk," Lizzie said. "The clerk told him you'd already paid for it and tried to show him another one, but he wanted yours." Lizzie frowned, snapped a glance at Sam. "He was a real jerk."

"What is Unclaimed Baggage?" Sam asked, sipping at his coffee.

"It's the only store like it in the country," Jaycee told him. "All the airlines send their unclaimed baggage there. They hold it for ninety days, then if it goes unclaimed, they sell it."

"As shopping goes," Lizzie said, "it's a pretty cool place. They have stuff there you'd never find anywhere else."

"I can't believe he was giving that clerk fits over my laptop."

"He didn't want another one." Lizzie glanced at Sam. "They had a whole bunch of them, but this guy was rabid. He wanted that one."

Jaycee wore her surprise all over her face. "I had no idea that's what he was angry about."

"The woman with the baby stood right next to you, Mom. I'd be shocked if you heard anything but the wailing." Lizzie's face turned serious. "The clerk who'd helped us motioned to the door, like he wanted us out of there before this guy left the counter. I think he worried he could follow us. He was kind of scary, the way he was acting." Lizzie frowned. "That's when I tugged you and said, "We have to go now.""

"I remember that. But I thought your shopping tolerance had just run out. You didn't say anything about any of this."

"Once we were gone, the problem was gone. Why dwell on it?" Lizzie shrugged.

Typical Lizzie. When it's over, it's over. Sam didn't know if that was a blessing or a challenge. He looked at Jaycee. "Why would anyone want that specific laptop? What's special about it?"

"Nothing." Jaycee lifted her hands. "They wipe the drive before they sell them, so there's nothing at all special about it."

Had to be something. Sam stroked his beard. "May I see it?"

"Sure." Jaycee left the table and then returned with the laptop. She passed it to Sam. "I can confirm it was wiped."

"If there's nothing on it, then there has to be something in it." Sam examined it on the tabletop, saw nothing unexpected. Then he opened the casing.

Jaycee gasped.

Lizzie gushed. "Wow!"

Taped to the inside rim of the outer casing was a USB drive. "Well, well," Sam said. "I think this is what the man wanted." Sam broke loose the tape and looked at Jaycee.

Her gaze narrowed to the USB drive. "That has to be what the stalker wants back."

Sam agreed.

"Let's see what's on it." Lizzie said, a gleam in her eye.

"I'll preview," Sam told her in a tone that brooked no argument. "Intense security on my phone." He plugged it in and then took a look at the USB drive contents.

Jaycee watched over his shoulder. "Oh, my word."

"What is it, Mom?"

"Numbers, baby. It's numbers." Jaycee looked at Sam. "Who keeps those kinds of records?"

He stared at the contents. "I'm no expert, but two potentials I've seen before come to mind. Feds or mafia."

Jaycee stiffened. "Feds would just have asked for it. Or gotten a warrant and taken it."

Sam nodded agreement. "Which leaves mafia."

"Great." Lizzie raised a frustrated hand. "Like we need somebody else chasing us."

"Take it easy, half-pint." Sam sent her a stony look.

"We can't just give it to the mafia," Lizzie said.

"No, but they will keep coming until they get it." Jaycee rubbed her hands together. "We have to turn it in."

Sam stroked his beard, thought through an idea on how to best handle this. "I've got this." He looked from Jaycee to Lizzie. "Pack a to-go bag. Enough to hold you over until after Christmas."

"Where are we going, Sam?" Lizzie asked, already on her feet.

"My house."

Lizzie lit up, totally thrilled. "Ooh, on the way can we talk about what you're going to add to Summerland?" Lizzie looked at her mother. "Sam's great-great grandfather built Summerland and every generation, the head of the house has to add something meaningful to it. Right, Sam?"

"That's right."

"It's a tradition." Lizzie yelled back, fleeing to the hallway to pack.

Lizzie had always loved Summerland. Appreciated its traditions and all his family stories. It was rich in history, and she'd especially loved all his 1800s memorabilia. The hours they'd spent talking about those things had been some of the best of his life.

Jaycee didn't move. She stammered. "I—I can't bring trouble to your home, Sam."

"You won't be." He smiled, which clearly confused her. "I have a plan."

CHAPTER NINE

December 22, 8:30 AM

While Jaycee and Lizzie were packing, Sam stepped onto the back porch, texted the photo of the arsonist and stalker to Mark, then called the office.

Mark answered.

"Perfect," Sam said. "Just the man I wanted."

"I take it the surveillance did some good."

"Yeah, it did," Sam said, staring at the burned-out hull of Jaycee's SUV. When he finished the call, he needed to run a thorough check on the truck. No way was he letting Jaycee or Lizzie anywhere near it until he knew the tracker was all that had been left behind and the arsonist hadn't tampered with anything. "You free to meet me at Summerland in two hours?" Sam asked. "I need a favor."

"You got it," Mark said. "The whole team or just me?"

"Just you."

"Okay." Mark hesitated, then asked. "Will you be arriving solo?"

Jaycee and Lizzie. Sam smiled. "No. Coming in heavy."

"Both?"

"Both."

"Awesome."

The line went dead.

Smiling to himself, Sam checked the truck.

Summerland
Hitch, Alabama
December 22, 9:45 AM

Mark sat in the kitchen waiting for them. Betsy, Sam's housekeeper, had come and gone but not before making a fresh pot of coffee, a tall pitcher of fresh lemonade, and serving Mark a slice of her infamous pecan pie. He was about halfway through it when Lizzie zoomed past Sam and Jaycee and grabbed Mark in a bear hug.

He laughed and wrapped his arms around her. "I knew I should have put a book on your head to keep you from growing so fast."

She grinned at him. "That wouldn't work, and you know I know it."

"Where's Betsy?" Lizzie asked Mark, looking for Sam's housekeeper.

"Don't worry. She's made up your room and one for your mother, and she's expecting Sam at her cottage come nightfall."

"She's at the cottage?"

Mark nodded at Lizzie. "She's got some cookies to bake for an in-gathering at church tonight. I bet she could use some help."

Sam stepped in. "Call Bob and let him know you're here and coming. You need the number?"

"I remember it." Lizzie pulled out her phone and dialed, excitement dancing in her eyes and filling her whole face.

Happy tears threatened Jaycee. Sam gave her arm a reassuring squeeze. Not once until now had he seen Lizzie carefree and happy.

Mark grinned. "Half-pint has always loved this place."

"She has." Jaycee gave Mark a quick hug. "It's good to see you."

"You, too." He smiled. "Sorry you've had a spot of trouble."

"I don't know why these things keep happening to me." She got herself a glass of lemonade and lifted a hand to Sam.

"Tea, please."

"Of course." Jaycee turned to snag another glass from the cabinet. She looked at home in his kitchen. He liked seeing her there.

"Appreciate you coming, Mark." Sam passed the USB drive. "That's the original. I don't have a copy."

"Okay."

Jaycee put Sam's tea near him on the table. Looked at Mark. "You want something cold?"

"No, thanks." He took a bite of pie, turned his gaze to Sam. "What is this?"

Sam briefed Mark.

"Whoa. A simple Girls Day Out sure stirred up a hornet's nest."

"Unfortunately, it's my gift." Jaycee sat down beside Sam.

"You asked why these things happen to you," Mark said. "I can tell you, if you like."

"I would like." Jaycee stared at him. "I've spent countless hours and days and years wondering."

"Because you're strong enough to handle them."

"What?"

"God needs things brought into the light. He uses people like you—and us—to do it."

"That sounds like a Nora-ism," Jaycee said.

"It is," Mark confessed. "Doesn't mean it isn't the truth. Nora is very wise."

"Yes, she is." Jaycee looked at Sam.

"Beats any reason I've got." He shrugged. "God asks. We all say yes. His will is done, and that's that."

Jaycee nearly smiled. "Well, why I didn't think of that, I have no idea. But I didn't."

"So, what's on this thing?" Mark tucked the USB drive into his pocket. "Do you know?"

"Mafia records for the feds, I think," Sam said. "Nick will know for fact, but that's our best guess."

"Okay."

"They're welcome to it," Sam said. "Actually, I want the feds to have it—but I do not want them to know Jaycee found it."

"Technically, you found it," Jaycee told Sam. "But I don't want you in any more jeopardy, so, Mark, it was in my laptop. Tell them that. It's the truth."

Sam sent Jaycee an uncompromising look. "You will not be involved in this."

"Wait. Stop, you two."

They paused their stare-down and focused on Mark. "This isn't a problem." Mark lifted his arms. "We are always confidential sources. Sam found it, gave it to me, and I gave it to them. Chain of custody secures the evidence. We're all set."

Sam nodded. "I wasn't thinking."

Mark stood up. "It happens. When those protective instincts engage, it's hard to think straight." He hugged Jaycee. "Glad you're back."

"Me, too," she said. "Even if it's just temporary."

Mark darted a glance to Sam, clapped him on the shoulder, then headed to the door.

"Let me walk you out," Sam said.

When they were halfway to Mark's Jeep, he turned to Sam. "It's none of my business, but—"

"You're going to butt in, anyway."

"Well, yeah. We're friends."

"And friends do that." Sam withheld a sigh. He'd been guilty of it himself. "Go ahead."

"You let that woman and Lizzie walk out once. You've been miserable without them. I know better than most you're a genius, but don't be dead-stump stupid and let them go again."

"That it?"

"Almost." Mark's expression softened. "We don't often get

second chances, Sam. You've been blessed with one here, and that's the truth. Think about that."

"I will."

Mark nodded and got in the Jeep. "I'll call when I have this handled—and when Nick IDs this guy. Could take a couple days, with everyone scattered for Christmas."

"Thanks, buddy."

Sam watched Mark drive away and saw Bob in the distance with Lizzie. They were on the dock at the lake. Lizzie sat on its edge, her feet swinging above the water. In her hand was a fishing rod. Sam smiled.

"What are you looking at?" Jaycee said from behind him.

"Lizzie. She knows this isn't the time of year for cork fishing."

Jaycee extended her gaze to her daughter. "That's not what she's doing," her mother said. "I mean, she is, but she isn't."

Sam looked at Jaycee. "She's reclaiming her home here."

Worry flitted through Jaycee's eyes. "I'm afraid she is. And when we leave, she's going to be heartbroken all over again."

"So, don't go."

Resignation slid over her face. "Sam, as much as that appeals, it's impossible."

"Why?"

"Because nothing has changed. I'm still a marked witness who puts you in more danger. NINA, Vargas's successor—they still want me dead, Sam. That won't stop so long as I'm alive, and we both have to accept it."

He wished he could argue the point. Tell her she was wrong. But she wasn't. If the danger were just on her side, things would be different. But PSC specialized in NINA and its messy problems. They had for a long time, so even selling out his interest with the partners wouldn't resolve the issue.

She clasped his arm. "Let's enjoy the time we have together, okay?"

A special Christmas for her and Lizzie would be something he could hold onto, remember for the rest of his life. "All right."

"Good."

If it was good, why did it feel so bad?

CHAPTER TEN

December 24, 2:30 PM

Christmas Eve morning, Sam and Jaycee had taken a long walk at Summerland. She had enjoyed going to Seagrove Village yesterday and visiting with Nora and Peggy, the Director at Crossroads Crisis Center. Jaycee and Lizzie had done some shopping, which is to say, a little shopping and a lot of visiting with old friends. Jaycee just fit here. In his world, in his life. And while he didn't want her to leave again, he couldn't ignore her observation about nothing having changed. People did still want her dead.

He'd thought about their situation, prayed on it, strained mightily and racked his brain for a solution but he'd failed to find one, and if God wanted him to have one, He hadn't yet shown it to Sam. He was trying to be still, reminded himself that God makes crooked places straight, and makes a way where there isn't one. But in the end, Sam found no solution, and he felt the weight of that failure. He wasn't just failing himself but failing Jaycee and Lizzie.

That hurt, pure and simple. He wanted nothing more than to succeed.

Some genius. Some security consultant. When he couldn't find a way that they could be together and protect her and Lizzie . . .

Deflated, he turned his collar to the wind and kept walking the land, hoping the answer he sought would come. Spotting the Summerland foreman, Bob, Sam ambled in his direction.

Bob promised Betsy he would remind Jaycee and Lizzie, who were squirreled away in their rooms upstairs wrapping presents, about the live Nativity program tonight, then reminded Sam that Betsy wouldn't be at the main house tomorrow because of it being Christmas. The older couple were as excited as Sam to have Jaycee and Lizzie back on the spread. Bob assured Sam he had Jaycee's gift all tucked away, safe and sound.

"You're positive she hasn't seen it?" Jaycee didn't miss much, and she'd spent half the morning outdoors, walking and looking over the winterized flowerbeds. The winter blooms she'd planted when here before had taken root and were blossoming, which made her happy. Sam was glad to see her happy and those dark circles under, and that haunted look in, her eyes fade away. He loved seeing that.

"No way, she's seen it." Bob eyes twinkled. "That beauty is in the barn and she's been nowhere near it. Nobody has but me."

"Why's it in the barn?" Sam asked.

Bob frowned at Sam. "So it's pristine come morning for the big reveal."

No self-respecting fleck of dust would dare mar the surprise for Jaycee under Bob's watch. "Right."

"Betsy went over to the flower shop and had a huge red bow made. We can't wait to see Jaycee's face."

"Me either. Thanks for everything, Bob." Sam nodded. Everyone wanted Jaycee and Lizzie to have a special Christmas. "I best get back."

"I'll have it there by dawn, in case Lizzie's up early." Bob grinned. "Wouldn't want to be late and see her disappointed even for a second."

Bob would be dozing until midnight then pacing and watching the clock, eagerly anticipating the time to move. Sam grinned. Giving was so much more fun than receiving. Watching them leave again, his failing them, was going to be a huge disappointment to a lot of people but to no one more than Sam. "Me, either." Never had truer words been spoken. Regret and resentment nipped at his heels already. "Thanks for your help," Sam said. "Thank Betsy, too."

"We're glad to do it." He turned away chuckling. "Gonna be a fine Christmas. Yes, sir, it is."

Sam hoped that proved true.

When he was about halfway back to the main house, he saw Lizzie running full-out toward him and hastened his steps. "Everything okay, half-pint?"

She was smiling, but she'd been smiling a lot lately. It had him edgy. Lizzie had always been so serious. Especially at the cabin. The smiles seemed genuine, but were they?

"Sam. Sam, I got an idea." She ran up to him and then stopped, her chest heaving from exertion.

Must be a doozy to have her this worked up. "An idea about what?"

She swiped the air with her hand. "I was brushing my teeth, not thinking about anything, and boom!"

"Boom?" He was trying to follow but totally lost. "What, boom?"

"Nothing exploded, except my idea." Impatient, she grabbed for his hand. "Come on. Just come with me."

"Where are we going?"

"To the river."

"It's way too cold to swim, half-pint."

"I know that. Come on, Sam. Please." Her enthusiasm rippled from her to him. "You are going to love this idea. Promise."

"Okay." He walked with her to the near bank of the river. It was pretty narrow through here. Maybe fifty yards wide and in a bend that Lizzie had a fondness for but never had said why. It was probably her favorite place on the whole spread. She used to come here to think, and he'd found her here more than once during their

Summerland visits, on her back, face to the sun, chewing on a long blade of grass.

She stopped and stared up at him. "Just to be sure nothing has changed, it's still Summerland property on the other bank, too, right?"

"Yes."

"For how far?" She squinted against the sun.

"Couple hundred acres," he said. "Maybe a little more. The property line stops down at the highway." He glanced from the distance to the river, and the flash of a memory of her in it, jumping up and down splashing, filled his mind. He tried to get her to swim in the lake, but she took exception to swimming in her favorite fishing hole. It disturbed the fish. A smile threatened Sam's lips. "What's this all about, Lizzie?"

"Give me just a second, okay?" She pressed a hand to her chest. "I want to think it through one more time. This is a big idea, Sam."

And important to her, gauging by her actions. "Okay. You take your time."

She paced a short path, checked angles, looked back to the lake near the dock, then back across the river to the other bank. Her eyes sparkled. "Okay, so. You know how every generation adds something to Summerland?" When he nodded, she went on. "Now, I know we tried to think of what you could add, but we came up dry."

"The right thing just hasn't come along. It's not just what is added, but what it means to those adding it, remember?"

"That was the part of the tradition stumping us." She stilled and her smile grew wide. "Well, I got it, Sam. I know exactly what you can add *and* what it means."

They'd talked about this all the way from the cabin, discussed a lot of possibilities, but none of them felt just right. "I'm all ears."

"A footbridge." Lizzie lifted her arm, pointed a finger at the river bend. "If you put it right here, then you stay dry going to the other side. No muddy boots."

"A footbridge." Sam stroked his beard, eyed the spot and imagined it. "That could come in handy." How many times growing up had his mother fussed about him tromping through here and then muddying up her floors? Hundreds.

Lizzie nodded. "Mom could plant some flowers on the bank flanking the head and the foot. It'd look really pretty. Pink flowers. Blue pink, not that bright pink, and purple ones, because of our code word." She spun around, her arms extended. "We'll be the only people in the whole world who know what the flowers mean."

"Your mom will know, too," he said, rolling the idea around in his head.

"She will. Just the three of us. She'll love that." Lizzie smiled. "Won't it be a glorious addition, Sam?"

He thought about it, but he didn't need to think. Lizzie was thrilled with the idea, and if it made her that happy, that had meaning for him. Every time he saw the flowers, he'd think of Jaycee. And the purple flowers, he'd think of Lizzie and Purple People-Eater. Others familiar with the tradition would consider it too simplistic, but he didn't care what they thought. He did care what she and Jaycee thought. "I believe it will." He rubbed his beard. "But I'll need help to do it. Since it's your vision, that should come from you."

Lizzie squealed and literally jumped up and down, hugging him while she was doing it. Sam couldn't help himself; he laughed, hard and deep.

"Thank you, Sam. I am really happy about the footbridge. It should be stone—for all the generations of Holts, past, present and future. Won't that be a great addition to Summerland? It's even more important since all your 1800s stuff isn't here anymore."

She still wasn't too happy about that. Hopefully, her opinion on it would soon change. "I like that—we can pick a color of stone for past, another for present, and a third for future Holts." He let his mind soak the meaning in deep. "It's a grand idea, Lizzie."

"Awesome. That's settled then." Lizzie backed away and her smile faded.

The change in her was stark. "What's wrong now, half-pint?"

"Nothing's wrong." She wrung her hands. "I guess, I'm a little nervous."

She was scared half out of her wits. "About what?"

After taking in a steadying breath, she lifted her gaze from his chest to his face. "I want to talk with you about something else, and it's important, too."

The footbridge was very important. She respected the place, its history and traditions. "Anything." He motioned for them to sit on the bank. When he was seated, he turned to her. "What is it?"

She sat down beside him. "There's no easy way to say this, so I'm just going to spit it out."

"One of your finest traits," he said. "Shoot."

"I need a dad," she said bluntly. "I've never had one. I mean, I did, but he died when I was a baby. All his family is gone. Anyway, I need a dad who's alive, and, well, I was wondering if you want the job?"

Before he could answer, she held up a hand. "I know having a kid is a big responsibility and having a teenager is not the easiest thing in the world. But I will try to not make it hard. I—I'm sure I'll mess up now and then, but I really will try to make sure you're not sorry." She blew out a puffed breath and stared at him as stiff as he'd ever seen her. "So, do you want the job?"

A knot settled in his throat that formed a boulder in his chest. "Honestly, I want that job more than my next breath," he admitted, dragging a thumb over her jaw.

"Then marry my mom. I know you love her."

"I do. More than life itself, and that's the truth," he said. "But marriage is a big thing, and she gets a say. Simple truth is I don't know if she loves me. She might not, half-pint."

Lizzie frowned at him. "You're kidding, right?"

He sobered. "No, I'm not kidding."

"Well, here's a clue." Lizzie leaned toward him and jabbed his ribs with her elbow. "She loves you."

His heart skipped a beat. Thudded hard. "Did she tell you that?" Not once had Jaycee ever said those words to him.

Lizzie rolled her eyes. "Ain't you been paying attention, Sam? She tells you every time she looks at you, or talks to you, or talks to anybody else about you."

Sam grunted. Mark had been right about talking to Lizzie. Who knew her mother better?

But Sam knew Jaycee too—well enough to know she would want to, but she wouldn't stay. He had to prepare Lizzie for that, because obviously, she wasn't considering leaving here. "Being your dad would be a privilege, but there's this problem of other people being after you two and after me."

"I seriously know that, okay? I live with it every day. That's never going to change. Bad people will always be after us." She lifted a pointed finger. "But here's the thing, and it's really simple. If they're after us all anyway, what's the difference?"

"I'm not tracking what you mean."

"Together or apart, they're coming. Well, we've been apart six years. It hasn't changed anything except, when things go south, we have to call you to come. So, if they're coming whether we're together or apart, why don't we face them together?" She pointed two fingers at her eyes. "More eyes on a problem better the odds in our favor, right? Saves you the trip to wherever we are, and we can help each other stay safe all the time."

He thought about it for a long minute. What she said was simple. It cleared the clutter and made total sense to him.

And there it was, the answer to his prayers, right there. *Thank you, God.* "Well now, ain't that something?"

"Sensible." Lizzie hiked her chin. "I'm a very sensible person. You've always said so."

"Beautiful and smart, too. And sensible."

The excitement returned to her eyes. "So, are you going to ask her?"

"I am, Lizzie." Sam smiled. "I don't know why I didn't see it that way before, but I do now, and so I definitely am."

"When?"

"Tomorrow."

Lizzie squealed again and hugged him hard. He loved those squeals. Sheer delight. "I am so going to love you being my dad."

"Hold on, now. I have to convince your mom, first. Don't get your heart set on her saying yes. She's very protective, Lizzie. Could be no matter what I say, she won't change her mind and stay or marry me."

"She will. I believe it." She tilted her neck in his direction. "You'll convince her, even without a white horse."

The memory of that exchange tickled him. "We got off to a rocky start, remember?" He kept a beefy arm wrapped around her slim shoulder. "You said I was no white knight."

"I did, and you aren't." Lizzie shrugged. "There was nothing rocky about that." She twined her pinky with his. "But I trusted you. Mom did, too. Right away."

That oddly disappointed him. "Is that why you want me to be your dad? Because you trust me to keep you safe?"

She stared at him a long second. "Wanting someone I didn't trust wouldn't be at all sensible, Sam."

"I'll be there for you and your mom either way. You know that."

"I do." She shrugged. "You always have been."

She'd once said she loved him. He'd been humbled. But had she meant it? "So, trusting me isn't the only reason you want me to be your dad?"

"Course not. Don't be foolish." She sounded like the village mother, Nora. "I love you, Sam, and I trust you."

She loved him. Warmth spread through his chest. A surge of happiness and love spread through him.

She tucked her hair behind her ear. "Since we're both new at this, you need to know something."

"Okay." He plucked up two blades of grass and passed her one, then tucked one into the corner of his mouth. "Shoot."

Lizzie rolled the blade between her finger and thumb, wearing her serious face, and looked right into his eyes. "A girl needs to know a dad loves her no matter what. Even if she's a hot mess."

"Her dad."

She nodded. "He'll even die for her." She stared at their hooked pinkies. "You did almost die for me and mom. Two times."

He didn't know what to say, so said nothing, just looked at this beautiful child who had long ago stolen his heart and given him a special place in hers.

She lifted her gaze. "But I've thought about this a lot, Sam. As important as being willing to die for me is, it's even more important to know that my dad will live for me. You'll live for my mom and me." She sniffed, rolled the blade between her fingers. "You taught me to fish, to know good snakes from bad ones, how to drive the lawn tractor, and swim and shoot—and you didn't go nuts when I mowed down the flowers. You took the blame." She straightened her shoulders. "That taught me I had to stand up and tell the truth. Not let you get blamed for something I did."

"I don't know what to say, Lizzie."

"Saying nothing is fine by me. You show me all the time what a girl needs to know. You'll die for me *and* you'll live for me, too. Even when I am not perfect—which is most of the time."

"I'll die and live for you as long as I'm able, Lizzie." He lifted their hooked pinkies. "Promise." Sam cleared his throat. "You know your dad didn't want to die and leave you, right?" When she nodded, he went on. "He loved you and your mother very much, and he fought hard to stay with you. But it was time for him to go. So, he did."

"Mom says it wasn't that he didn't want me. But I have wondered . . ."

"Don't. He loved you, Lizzie. You were his daughter. No way did he want to leave you."

"My heart knows that, but now and then my head tries to convince me otherwise."

"Well, let's get this settled between you and me right now. You know my work is dangerous."

"I know. I remember Costa Rica. You could have been killed. And you do that kind of stuff a lot, helping people." She swallowed hard. "I'm not crazy about it. Mom isn't either. It scares us. But if you hadn't come when we needed help, we wouldn't be here. I think about that a lot, too."

"I can't promise not to die, Lizzie. I can promise to love you like you're my daughter because, in my heart, you are my daughter. For as long as I live, I'll love you and your mother."

"If she'll marry you."

"Either way."

Looking very pleased by that, she nodded. "Can't ask for more than that." Lizzie stood up, then focused on him. "As long as I'm breathing, I'll love you, too, Sam. Even after, if I can. Promise."

He gained his feet and dusted off his seat. "This footbridge . . . it's important to you."

"Very," Lizzie said.

"Why?" He thought he understood, but he wanted to be sure.

"It's respecting the past and present and ties all Holts to the future. They'll walk that bridge forever." She shrugged. "I love that, Sam."

Put like that, he did, too.

"Tradition is important, especially if you don't have any of your own. Old ones are all over this land. And the bridge builds new ones." She lifted her face, her expression dreamy. "Summerland and us just continuing on and on."

Her answer pleased him immensely. Moving place to place, leaving everything behind and starting over, traveling light and all the safety measures . . . she longed for the stability and security of tradition. That anchor he could give to her and to Jaycee—if she'd have him.

"You want me to work on Mom about this marriage thing?"

"Absolutely not." He stroked his beard. "I want to do it myself." At least if she broke his heart about it, he would have a little time to glue himself together before facing Lizzie with the bad news.

Oh, but he hoped Lizzie was right, and Jaycee did still love him. She had said at the cabin, if he had asked her to stay, she would have said yes.

Then.

But this wasn't then, it was now. What would she say now?

Didn't he wish he knew?

CHAPTER ELEVEN

December 25th, 6:00 PM

Jaycee stood at the Christmas tree, looking at the ornaments that had been collected over the last five generations of Holts. "This collection is awesome, Sam."

"Holts have a rich heritage." Lizzie sat on the floor at the coffee-table across from Sam on the sofa, sitting arms on knees, staring at the Monopoly board.

Holts did. After their talk earlier, he'd never take that heritage for granted again. "I concede, half-pint. Unless I roll twenty-six, which isn't possible, you've got me." He passed over his cash and deeds. "Congratulations."

"Woohoo!" Lizzie laughed. "First time I've ever beaten you at this." She shot him a suspicious look. "You didn't let me win, did you?"

"I'm sorry to say, I did not. You beat me, fair and square."

Lizzie bounced on her knees. "I need some tea."

Jaycee turned. "Too late in the day for that."

Lizzie looked at Sam's glass on the coaster. "It's Christmas. Please, Mom."

"All right. But just a little glass."

Lizzie turned so her mom couldn't see her face and whispered to Sam. "Would you just do it?" She added an eye roll he didn't need. "I've been waiting all day."

Frankly, so had he, but every time he was ready and looked at Jaycee, he stopped short. If she refused, he'd be wrecking their Christmas, and it had been a perfect day. The best any of them had had in years.

Lizzie had been so excited about the tickets for a private tour of the museum where the Holt memorabilia was housed. She was every bit as crazy as he about the stuff. And when Bob had rolled out the SUV, Jaycee had been overwhelmed. It was white with dove gray interior. Sam had told her if she'd prefer a different color, they could switch it out. She'd pressed her fingertips over his lips and looked up at him with tears in her eyes. "I love the color," she'd said. "But it's way too expensive a gift." He'd nixed that objection with assurances he wanted her to have it.

Looking on, Bob and Betsy hadn't been disappointed. Jaycee had hugged and kissed him right there on the spot.

Lizzie went to the kitchen for her tea, and Jaycee sat down beside him on the sofa. "This has been an absolutely beautiful Christmas, Sam. Thank you."

"Thank you."

"All day, I've been waiting for the phone call from Mark that blows it all apart. But it hasn't come." She rolled her head against the back of the sofa to look at Sam. "Resolving the mafia's USB drive can't be this easy, can it?"

"We'll have to see." He hoped, but he didn't dare bank on it and disappoint her.

"It can't." She shrugged. "It never is. There's always a catch. These kinds of problems never just disappear."

She was right. Typically, they didn't. But that didn't mean they couldn't, especially with a little help from PSC. "It doesn't hurt to have confidential source status and a long history with these people." Sam patted her arm. "Mark's got this. We just need to be patient and see what he works out."

Jaycee nodded, flipped her auburn hair back from her face. It caught the lights from the Christmas tree. "Be right back. There's a piece of fudge in the kitchen with my name on it. You want one?"

"No, thanks." If he tried to swallow right now, he'd choke.

Lizzie shuffled over to him. "Will you just do it? You said Christmas, and it's already dark outside."

He was nervous, but he nodded at Lizzie. All he needed was to put himself out there and get stomped. "Okay, okay." He blew out a deep breath. "Give me a second."

"She's coming back. Just do it, Sam. It'll be great." Lizzie snagged Jaycee's phone and went back into the kitchen.

On Jaycee's way back, she spotted a clothespin reindeer like the one Lizzie had made in kindergarten hanging on the tree. Smiling, she stroked it. "Did you make this?"

"No, it's Lizzie's."

"You hung her ornament on the Holt tree?"

Was Jaycee upset? Unsure, he nodded. "She loves the Holt ornaments as much as me. Hers should hang with them."

Jaycee gave him a slow blink. "That's a beautiful gesture. I'm sure it means a lot to her, and it does to me."

"It's only right."

Jaycee looked to him to explain. He didn't. Instead, Sam stood up. "Can we talk about something important?"

"Sure." She smiled.

Sam stroked his beard. "Well, um, I've been thinking."

Her smile wobbled. She had no idea what was on his mind. "Oh, no. You heard from Mark and it's bad news."

"No, I didn't." He rubbed at his neck, stepped closer. "You remember what we talked about at the cabin?"

"The case?"

"No." This was harder than he thought. "Our talk about marriage."

"I remember, yes." The smile disappeared.

Was that a sign? He studied her. She looked a little apprehensive and a little scared. Not exactly what he'd been hoping for, but while he'd worried about how she felt, he now understood she had no idea how he felt.

His phone rang. Priority ringtone. And distant. "Sorry, I have to get that." He followed the ring to the kitchen, not recalling leaving his phone in there.

Lizzie stood near the fridge, holding two phones. One was his. She passed it to him.

"Thanks." He listened. "Hello."

"Sam, it's Mark. The mafia Christmas Stocking stalker is in custody."

"That's good news."

"Kind of fits with Christmas and everything," Mark said. "Anyway, his boss was not happy that he'd lost his laptop—the guy at Unclaimed Baggage. He was even less happy that the feds found the USB drive, and he's really unhappy now that he and Mafia Boss have been arrested. But our guys are very happy. Apparently, they've been trying to get Mafia Boss for a long time. They were primed and ready, just waiting for something like that drive."

"Who is he?" Sam asked, leaning a hip against the island.

"That's best left undisclosed."

Mark was right about that. "And she isn't mentioned."

"Not once. To anyone beyond you and me."

Relief flooded through Sam. "Thanks, buddy."

"Anytime." Mark cleared his throat. "Okay, the team's all here and we're waiting to hear Jaycee's reaction. When you asked her, what'd she say?"

Lizzie had told them. Sam's mouth went dry. "Nothing yet."

"He chickened out." Nick groused on Mark's end in the background. "You did, didn't you?"

"No," Sam said. "You interrupted."

"He's delayed all day," Tim said. "It's night already. Get it done, Sam."

He sounded like Lizzie.

Mark grunted. "I know Lizzie didn't oppose."

"No. I was just easing into it when you called."

"You're endangering our marital bliss, bro. There's no way we can keep our wives on hold much longer," Joe said. "You need help?"

"No."

"It's Nick, Sam. Remember that special favor you asked me to do?"

"Yeah."

"Well, get this done. It's ready and waiting, and they're understandably anxious."

"Secure on both ends?"

"Absolutely," Nick said.

"Thanks, buddy."

"No thanks needed. Just get this done and get to it."

A very special Christmas surprise for Jaycee. "Right." Sam paced a short path in the kitchen between the island and a row of cabinets. He clenched the phone. "Right."

A guilty-looking Lizzie stood near the fridge, watching him. The guys cheered him on. Well, except for Nick. "Otherwise, we could all come to Summerland," Nick said, "and help you out, or even do it for you. You know, if you can't handle the mission."

Joe growled. "Stop, Nick. Don't even think about it, Sam. Trust me, bro. That is not the way you want to go on this."

"What is?" Sam asked.

"Truth. Honesty. Be sincere."

"I can do that." He could. They'd always been honest with each other.

"Good. Report in when the mission is accomplished and you're ready for the big surprise." Mark ended the call.

Lizzie shooed him back into the living room. "Hurry, Sam. You're running into a different time zone."

"All right." Sam plunked his phone down on the island and went back to Jaycee.

She lifted an eyebrow, clearly curious. "Everything okay?"

From the corner of his eye, Sam spotted Lizzie peeking around the corner. Was she holding two phones up in the air? Amusing herself, he supposed. Not much to do in the kitchen.

"Sam?" Jaycee looked worried now.

"It's done," he said plainly, "and you were never mentioned, so you're not involved."

"But the guy knew I had it."

"And you never knew it. I found it, and I gave it to Mark. Now the feds have it and the Christmas Stocking stalker and Mafia Boss are under arrest."

Relief flooded her face. "That's wonderful. I can't quite believe it, but it's wonderful."

Lizzie twirled her finger for him get on with it. Sam couldn't blame her. This was her life, too, and she was eager to live it on her terms.

Jaycee looked away. "I guess we can go back to the cabin then."

She didn't sound happy. His hopeful heart raced. "I want you to stay. You and Lizzie being here . . . Well, it's the first time in a long time Summerland has felt like home."

"I'm sorry."

He frowned. "That was a compliment."

"That you've been lonely is a compliment?"

"I haven't been lonely. Well, not generally speaking. I have been missing you."

"We miss you too, Sam."

He steeled himself. Gritted his teeth. "The thing is, Jaycee, I messed up six years ago." He met and held her gaze. "I'm not going to mess up again."

"What do you mean?"

He dropped to a knee, reaching in his pocket for the ring—and came up empty. It was on the island. He wiggled his fingers at his back.

Lizzie came running, dropped the box in his hand, then ran back to the kitchen.

"This time," Sam said, "I'm asking, Jaycee."

She gasped.

He rushed to get the words out. "Marry me. Build a life with me here. You and Lizzie mean the world to me, and I don't want to lose you again."

She stroked his upturned face. "Sam, I get being lonely. I am, too. And it has to be harder now that all the partners are married."

"The guys have nothing to do with this—and I'm not lonely. I miss you and Lizzie."

"The guys do have something to do with this. You used to do everything together and now all that's changed. They have families and you're still alone. But loneliness is no reason to marry."

"Couldn't agree more. It isn't. Not for either of us." He softened his voice. "Truth is, I love you, Jaycee. I have since the first time I saw you. And I love Lizzie."

"I know you do." Jaycee blinked hard and fast, afraid to believe. "But we've been through this before and the risks haven't changed, Sam."

"I didn't think they had, either. But fact is, things are different." He went on to share Lizzie's wisdom from the river.

"That sounds like Nora talking."

"Lizzie," he confessed. "She probably got some of it from Nora, but it's her, too. And she's right."

"You really think so?" Hope filled Jaycee's face. "Seriously?"

"I do. And I'm six years' worth of sure what we've been doing apart isn't working. Together has got to be better."

"Be really certain, Sam, because if it doesn't work, it will kill me and Lizzie."

"It'd kill me, too." His throat went tight. "Take a chance with me, Jaycee. That is, if you love me."

"I love you." She cupped his face in her hands. "That's never been the problem. I've always loved you."

Forty tons of worry slid right off his broad shoulders. "Then marry me."

"Okay, I will."

He stood up, and she wrapped her arms around him. He kissed her, letting her feel the depth of emotion she stirred in him he had such a hard time translating into words.

Lizzie couldn't contain herself. "Yes! Yes! Yes!" She squealed into the phone.

Sam and Jaycee turned their attention to her, and Lizzie's face turned bright red. "Sorry." She stood there with a phone in each hand, holding them up toward the living room. "I'm excited."

The reason for the phones, he now understood. "You let them listen in?" Sam looked at Jaycee. "The guys."

"Course." Lizzie saw the reprimand in their expressions and whispered into the phone. "I, um, gotta go now." She paused. "Yep, totally busted."

To a round of laughter and applause, Lizzie set both phones on the island. "Um, we're all excited." She dropped pretending to be contrite, rushed to her mother and Sam and sandwiched herself between them in a heartfelt hug. "This is absolutely the best Christmas ever!"

They all laughed, and Sam asked, "Just out of curiosity, who was on the second phone?"

Lizzie's jaw went slack. "Nora!" She ran back to the kitchen and lifted it. Clearly, Nora was on speaker. "Nora, are you still there?"

"Me miss this?" Nora laughed. "Not a chance."

"Oh, isn't it awesome, Nora?"

"It is. Now ask your mama when she wants the wedding."

Lizzie relayed and Jaycee strolled over and took the phone. "We'll get back to you on that, Nora."

Sam stepped forward. "Ask her how soon they can put it together. I don't want to wait."

"You know what? I agree," Jaycee said. "We've already waited long enough."

Nora heard. "Tomorrow at three. Be at the chapel at Cross-roads. Annie and I figured it best, being your special place and all."

Sam frowned. "You want to get married in the chapel at the crisis center?"

"Would you mind?" Jaycee worried her lip with her teeth. "I love that chapel. And we did meet there."

"Works for me." Sam shrugged.

"Tomorrow?" It hit Jaycee. "We can't get a license—"

"We got friends," Nora insisted. "We'll get it."

"But I don't have a dress—" Jaycee paused, listened. "Oh, okay, I'll expect her in the morning, then."

A few minutes later, Jaycee ended the call. "Everything I brought up, they've already handled."

"Annie and Nora are the world's best wedding planners," Lizzie said. "They think of everything."

"I can't believe it," Jaycee said. "We're getting married tomorrow at three."

"Well, ain't that something?" Sam smiled and hugged Jaycee. Over her shoulder, he winked at Lizzie. How long she'd been working on this with Nora, he had no idea, but that she had been was written all over her face. He silently mouthed, "Thanks, half-pint."

She beamed.

Jaycee whispered against his chest. "You realize we've been set up, right?"

"Oh, yeah," he whispered back. "And I'm grateful for it." He pulled back, put his great-great grandmother's ring on Jaycee's finger.

She gushed. "It's perfect."

Sam accepted butterfly kisses to his face. He might just kind of love them. "You up for one more surprise?"

"I'm already overwhelmed. Sam, you've done . . ."

Lizzie horned in. "You'll like this one, Mom. Just say yes."

"It's a day of miracles." Jaycee hunched her shoulders. "Yes."

Sam nodded to Lizzie, who spoke into the phone. "Nick, you ready?"

"Ready."

Lizzie tapped for Face Time. "Mom, this is a Christmas present for you from me. Sam and Nick helped. I'm supposed to tell you that the call is encrypted and secure. It's safe for everyone involved."

Lizzie passed her mother her telephone.

Jaycee took it, glanced at the screen, and burst into tears that streamed down her face. "Mom? Dad?"

And the waterworks and chattering of an unexpected and long-awaited reunion began.

Sam's own eyes burning, he smiled at Lizzie. "Well done, half-pint."

"Thanks for helping me." She cocked an eyebrow at him. "When you said anything, anytime, anywhere, you weren't kidding."

Jaycee was already on her third tissue. "This was just what your mom needed. Exactly."

"This and you." Lizzie looked up at him. "This together thing is working out great so far, isn't it?"

"Better than great."

"Well, since we're on a roll and you're going to be my dad, I think you should consider adopting me. Make it official with me, too."

"Okay—if your mom agrees, I mean."

"Really?" Lizzie's whole face lit up.

"I meant what I said, half-pint. In my heart, you've been my daughter a long time."

"Well, why didn't you say so?" Lizzie parked a hand on her hip. "Mom made Ben and Kelly and Crossroads Crisis Center my guardians a long time ago. You know, just in case something happened to her. But she also said, if at any time you wanted to adopt me, she approved, and it was to be done."

Sam felt poleaxed. "She did?"

"Yeah, she did. They've got papers and everything." Lizzie tilted her head. "When you got us out of Costa Rica . . . Remember how you held me that whole flight, and I was upset because they'd smeared motor oil on my hair, so it'd be harder to see in the moonlight?"

"I remember." It'd made his blood boil.

"I wanted it off."

"You said it felt like slime."

"You washed my hair with bottles of water and soap, even though that plane guy got mad at the mess. You told him to back off, and the team stood up and blocked him. He didn't think about taking them on, just went away. You washed my hair like it was the most important thing in the world to you." Her sweet face went more serious. "That's when I knew only you could ever be my dad."

"I didn't know that." Sam's throat felt thick.

"I told Mom, and she promised to fix the papers so if you ever asked, Ben and Kelly would let you adopt me. Kelly told me Mom had."

Sam looked Lizzie right in the eye. "I'm asking," he said. "If I'd known, I'd have asked a long time ago."

"Why?"

"Because I love you, Lizzie. And, I have to say, because nobody loves Summerland like me and you. You've got more Holt in you than—"

She gasped and her eyes filled with tears she blinked to conceal. "That means all your traditions will be my traditions?"

Knowing how much that mattered to her, he choked up but managed a nod.

She sniffed and wrapped her arms around him. "I love you so much." Lifting her chin, she promised. "I'm going to make you proud of me, Sam."

"I am proud of you."

"Prouder. I love Summerland and I always will. That's a promise."

So earnest. So sincere. It mattered more than even he realized. Lizzie belonged. "I know you do. Always have, and that bridge we're going to build, it's going to be Lizzie Holt's Bridge, so everybody knows you added something significant to Summerland."

"But the tradition has to be something you added."

Sam stroked his beard. "I am adding something. The most significant thing in the world to me." His eyes glossed. "You and your mom."

Her lips curved in a liquid smile. "I said this is the best Christmas ever, but it's really the best *ever* ever."

"For me, too, half-pint." He said and meant it. "For me, too."

Jaycee and her parents were still talking, and she was laughing at something her mother had said. Standing near Jaycee, Lizzie laughed with them, and watching them Sam sighed, a contented man.

In the years ahead, as crazy as it might sound to someone who hadn't lived it, he figured he'd continue to owe a debt of gratitude to the Christmas Stocking stalker. And a couple serious debts to Lizzie. Who could have imagined?

Why he was surprised at this amazing turnaround in life, he couldn't figure. He had seen unexpected resolutions time and time again, though most had been in other people's lives. But God had a way of taking something intended for harm and turning it into something good. Something wonderful. And He did that a lot.

Things like bringing Jaycee and Lizzie back into Sam's life, and giving them all a third chance after they'd blown the first two chances. Like using Lizzie as a messenger to point out the obvious that both he and Jaycee had missed. Things like sparing Jaycee from another traumatizing, life-altering event that left her with yet another scar as the marked witness . . .

Jaycee got off the phone, squealed and hugged Lizzie. "That was an amazing gift, Lizzie. Thank you so much." She looked to Sam. "And thank you for helping Lizzie do that. I needed to talk to my folks—and they needed to hear from us just as much."

Never had he seen Jaycee or Lizzie so happy. Never. Inside, he melted, and opened his arms. Jaycee and Lizzie rushed into them, laughing through tears, mumbling words he couldn't make out but understood down deep. And he whispered a silent thank you. By the grace of God, their family circle was finally complete.

SNEAK PEEK: THE MARKED BRIDE

Please enjoy this Sneak Peek of *The Marked Bride*, Book 1 in the
Shadow Watchers series

CHAPTER ONE

Thursday, October 16th
Maddsen, Florida

The grocery bag slipped.

Mandy pivoted on the sidewalk to keep from dropping it and, at
the curve, spotted a flood of police cars in the street in front of her
mother's house. Her heart rate shot up. Her pulse throbbing in her
throat, in her temple, she ran toward them, cut across the lawn,
veered onto the walkway to the wide front porch, and then climbed
up the bottom step.

A uniformed police officer in his fifties raised his hand, blocked
her path. "Stop. You can't go in there, ma'am."

Mandy shook her shoulder, trying to shoot past him, letting the
grocery bag bump against his chest. "Of course, I can go in."

"Detective Walton." He called out then motioned for a man in a gray suit to join him. "Over here."

"Yeah, Hank." The detective said to the officer.

Out of patience and fighting panic, Mandy interrupted. "What are you people doing here?" She let her gaze slide between the two men, hoping one of them would answer her. The detective was a good ten years younger than the uniformed officer but looked far more rumpled, worn and weary.

A guard slid down over the detective's eyes. "Do you know Olivia Dixon?"

"Yes, I know her. She's my mother." Mandy frowned at him. "What's going on? Why are you here—and *where* is my mother?"

"I'm Detective Walton. Maddsen P.D." He reached for the two grocery bags she'd forgotten she held. "Let me take those for you. Why don't you sit down, Miss . . .?"

She instinctively passed the bags. "Madeline Dixon—Mandy," she said, a sinking feeling dragging at her stomach, broadening the growing fissure of fear inside her. All around them, officers went in and out of the house. One rushing past brushed against her back, mumbled an apology, but didn't slow his steps. "No more questions. I want you to take me to my mother. Are you going to do it or not?"

"I can't take you to her right now, Miss Dixon." Regret flashed through Walton's eyes and his tone softened. "Won't you sit down here on the step? Please."

If she didn't, he'd tell her nothing. Clear on that much, Mandy sat down on the rough, top concrete step. "Is something wrong with her?" *No. Please, no. Not her. Please, not her.* "Is she sick?" She couldn't let herself think anything worse. This many cops didn't show up for someone sick, but she couldn't wrap her mind around more.

"We didn't know who to call." Walton passed the bags to the uniformed officer, then sat down beside Mandy on the top step. "None of the neighbors knew her or your name, though some had seen a woman fitting your description come and go from here."

Of course, she wasn't sick. Something bad had happened. Cops swarmed like bees all around her, and one was stretching yellow crime-scene tape between the trees separating her yard from the next-door neighbor's. Something wickedly bad. "She's lived here a relatively short time—maybe a year."

"A year, and none of her neighbors know her?" He clearly found that odd.

"Mom has always kept to herself." *She's a recluse for good reason.* Mandy shunned the thought, vowing she wouldn't whisper another word until he told her what had happened. She stared at him, and then waited . . . and waited.

Realizing she would stay clammed up, he shifted on his concrete seat, resigned. "I'm sorry, Miss Dixon. There's no easy way to say this. I wish there were." Regret flashed through his eyes, genuine and sincere. "Your mother is dead."

The bottom dropped out of her stomach. "Dead?" He had to be mistaken. Wrong. *Dead? Impossible.* "No. No, you've made some kind of mistake. She can't be dead." Mandy disputed him and shunned the shock pumping through her body. "We just talked a few hours ago. We're having dinner together here tonight. I'm cooking. I—I brought the groceries."

"There's no mistake." Walton spoke slowly, distinctly, giving Mandy time to absorb his words. "Your mother is dead. I'm so sorry for your loss, Miss Dixon."

"No," she insisted. "I talked to her. We're having lasagna and a Caesar salad—"

Walton didn't dispute her, just continued on. "The neighbor across the street called." He pointed to the white house trimmed in yellow, one house over and opposite her mother's. The neighbor who'd had an insane amount of flowers in her front yard last summer. "She was out winterizing her flowerbeds, heard shots fired, and phoned us. We responded right away, but we arrived too late. We found your mother inside the house. The coroner is with her now."

Her mother? Dead? Dead. Oh God, dead! No. No . . . No! Spots formed before her eyes and her stomach pitched. Hot and cold at once, she broke into a clammy sweat and her trembling intensified to shaking. Her world tilted and fighting to clear her head, she screamed inside.

Outwardly, she took a moment and then forced cold-steel calm into her voice. "If you're telling me she killed herself, you're wrong. My mother would never do that." She might want to; heaven knew she'd threatened to often enough over the years, but she wouldn't do it for the same reason she never had: she wouldn't deliberately leave Mandy alone in the world.

"No." Walton let his gaze slide away. "She didn't . . . hurt . . . herself." He dragged his gaze to Mandy's. "It's clear to us," he said, and then paused as if seeking the right words. Apparently deciding he wouldn't find any, he leveled his tone and went on. "Your mother was murdered."

More shock. More pain. A full-out assault. *Murdered.* Mandy hissed in a sharp breath, and then another. And then yet another. Her mother was dead. *Murdered?* "By who? She didn't associate with anyone but me."

"That's what we have to try to figure out." Walton looked past his shoulder to the uniformed officer he'd called Hank. "Time the grocery receipt."

"Yes, sir."

Walton returned his focus to her. "I really am sorry, Miss Dixon." He blinked hard and fast. "You shouldn't be alone. Is there anyone I can call for you?"

Tim's image filled her mind and her heart shattered yet again. She wanted and needed him, but she couldn't call him. "Give me a minute to think. Just a minute to think." Scanning her mind, she thought of her father. She *definitely* couldn't call him. He'd never forgive her.

She had learned young that she could never contact him under any circumstances. That no matter how hard she wished or prayed he might be like other fathers, he wasn't and he never would be, and he certainly would never be a dad to her—not like other dads. Every single day in each of her twenty-eight years, she'd had no choice but to accept those facts and to live with them. Neither he, nor her mother, had ever permitted her to harbor any fantasies. No, she couldn't call him. But when he heard about her mother, he would be devastated.

At least, Mandy thought he would. *Please, let him be devastated. Please.*

The idea of her mother sacrificing all she had and him not being devastated inflicted more pain than Mandy could bear.

"Any other family?" Detective Walton asked. "A grandmother or cousin?"

Biting her lip, she nodded that there wasn't any. Bitterness settled in her stomach. Her father had always kept them isolated.

"What about a friend?" Walton asked, lacing his fingers and draping his arms between his knees.

Again, she nodded negatively. Friends were for families not keeping secrets.

"Detective, excuse me. I need to see you inside."

He lifted a finger at the man, then looked at Mandy. "I'll be right back. If you need anything, just tell Hank."

Mandy nodded and watched the detective ease inside. He must have signaled Hank. He kept his distance at the edge of the porch, but stood watching her.

They were suspicious of her. She couldn't blame them, but that too, was her father's fault. Dirty secrets required distance, silence, staying apart.

She sought solace. Her father would be devastated at losing her mother. He had loved her. Even as a child, on his Tuesday visits, Mandy had picked up enough evidence of that to never doubt it. He'd always been a part of their lives, but they never really had been a part of his life. He'd never lived with them, or been the husband her mother deserved, or the father that her mother claimed Mandy deserved, but he'd loved her mother, and for reasons clear only to her, she had loved him.

And how that grated at Mandy.

Charles Travest might be a high-powered attorney and he might have every single material trapping that went with it, but all he had ever shared with her mother had been money and leftover crumbs of affection. With Mandy, he had shared even less.

Not once in her whole life had he ever said he loved her. Sometimes when he looked at her, she thought he might. But then he'd say, "You remind me so much of your mother" or "You look more like your mother every day," and Mandy had known. It wasn't her he saw or loved. His feelings for her were, in his own strange way, an extension of his love for her mother. Nothing more. Mandy surmised long ago she had been, was, and would never be anything more to him than an inconvenient complication.

At seventeen, when the truth revealed itself in all its sordid ugliness, her theory proved fact. Until then, she'd tried to win his affection by being clever and witty. She hadn't succeeded, though now and then, he had found her amusing. Starved for anything, his amusement had seemed like a lot to her hungry heart. At least it had, until the event. That day, everything had changed forever.

She'd seen him in St. Augustine. He'd passed her on the street and looked right through her as if he'd never before in his life seen her. He hadn't been alone . . . and Mandy had discovered the truth about him.

Later, her mother had confirmed Mandy's deductions, and that was that . . . until Mandy had met Tim Branson three years ago.

The conversations going on around her faded to a dull drone of voices, and she let herself find comfort in her memories.

Tim Branson. From the very beginning, Tim *saw* her. Outside and inside. He'd walked into her jewelry store, charming and sophisticated, approachable and emotionally wide open. He spoke his mind, and his honesty arrowed right into her heart.

When he had invited her to dinner, no one had been more surprised. Lured by his openness, his straight talk, Tim fascinated her. So much so that she ignored her better judgment warning her that, while he was nothing like her father, men like Tim were never seriously interested in women like her and she had to keep everyone distant, and she accepted the invitation.

One dinner turned into another and then another. He listened to her dreams. Looked at her with tenderness and truth. He trusted and cherished her, sought her opinions, and respected her ideas. When he told her he loved her the first time on a walk through town square, he became the one man in her life that she knew with total and complete certainty did love her.

That was far more precious to her than all the diamonds and jewels in her well-stocked store.

Detective Walton returned to her, still sitting quietly on the step. He looked concerned and even more weary. "You didn't call anyone?"

"No."

A nodding Hank confirmed that, and Walton looked back at her, almost desperate. "Surely there's someone I can call for you, Mandy."

Tim.

Memories flooded her, stacked and tumbled and shattered. Her heart squeezed her chest tight. Her eyes filled with tears that blurred her vision. His proposal had stunned her—still stunned her. At the time, she'd been beyond stunned. Awed. Awed and, in her eyes, witnessing a miracle. *He* wanted to spend his life with *her*? She challenged him. *Men like you don't marry women like me. You marry women who have it all.*

You have it all.

I don't. I—I She'd looked away. *There are things about me you don't know.*

There are things about me you don't know, too. We'll learn together.

It took him a while, but he'd convinced her. She was *the one* for him.

And heaven knew he had been the one for her. No one touched her heart, captivated her like Tim. No one else ever had, or would again.

An ache hollowed her heart. They would have been married —*should have been married*—now. But she'd been warned off. Persuasively. Permanently. Irrevocably. And so she'd done the hardest thing she'd been asked to do in her life. She'd walked away from Tim and closed the door on his love.

She had regretted that decision since the moment she'd made it.

Now, she regretted it even more.

She looked directly into the detective's eyes. "No. There is no one to call." Her throat went tight and her chest felt squeezed. "Not anymore."

Tim was a former Shadow Watcher—one of the secrets about himself he revealed after she had accepted his proposal. A spy who spied on spies. He was part of a team of them and, after an incident, the details of which he had not shared, his entire team had left active-duty and had started their own private-security consultant firm. They—Tim—could find out who had murdered her mother.

She considered reaching into her purse for the secure phone they always had used to talk. It never rang anymore; it hadn't since she'd broken their engagement. But she couldn't make herself put the phone away or get rid of it and break their final physical connection. She'd tried—many times—but she just couldn't do it anymore than she could stop loving him.

Temptation escalated to an urge to phone him and it fired through her with the force of a physical blow. She absorbed that, too, and then the successive series of urges that followed, denying them all. She couldn't call Tim any more than she could call her father. After what she'd done to him? Knowing what could happen? No. No, she had no right . . .

Resignation slid onto her like a heavy coat. With a sigh, she faced Detective Walton, who sat patiently, giving her time to fight her way through the first wave of emotional turmoil his news had triggered. "No, but thank you for your kindnesses. There's no one to call. It's always been just my mother and me."

"What about co-workers?" Walton pushed. "Employees?"

That stung. "Yes, I have employees, but they are not involved in my personal life."

"What about neighbors from an old neighborhood?" He frowned, either not believing her or surprised. "Surely you and your mother interacted with someone."

Charles Travest. The idea of disclosing him flitted through her mind, but the potential consequences halted her. It would only cause more pain. She'd been on the receiving end of that pain in St. Augustine. No way would she willingly inflict the nightmare on another. He might have sacrificed her, but responsibility for that rested on his head. She wouldn't sacrifice him or destroy his life. "Afraid not. There's no one."

Her chest ached with shame and embarrassment. In Walton's line of work, he'd seen and heard it all, and clearly he thought their isolation was odd. She agreed with him, but she couldn't admit it.

"I'm sorry." Walton said and meant that, too. Pity burned in his eyes.

When seeing it stopped putting spasms into her throat, she swallowed hard. "I want to see my mother."

"Soon. But I can't allow that right now." He glanced down at Mandy's feet, avoiding her eyes. "We're still gathering evidence."

She'd contaminate the crime scene. "I understand." Protecting the scene, she could grasp. Her mother being dead just didn't make sense. "You, personally, are certain it's her?"

"I am. I found her driver's license in her handbag. There's no doubt."

Dead. Her mother was dead. Why?

Immediately, Mandy's mind went to the threats against Tim. But surely not. She'd done exactly what she'd had to do and hadn't heard a word about it since then. There had been no contact. None. No, this couldn't be about him. It had to be unrelated.

"I know it is terrible to bother you with questions, but time isn't on our side. If we're going to stand a chance of catching whoever did this . . ."

Get it together, Mandy. Clear your mind. Focus. "I understand. Go ahead."

"You say there was no one else, so I have to ask." His voice softened. "Did you kill your mother?"

"What?"

"I have to ask," he repeated. "It's my job, Mandy."

"I told you. It's been her and me my whole life." Mandy looked him right in the eye, let him see her pain. *Alone. Vulnerable. Lost. Empty.* "She was all I have." Her broken heart shattered again. "No, Detective. I didn't kill her."

His expression didn't alter. "Where were you at about six tonight?"

Routine questions? Or he suspected her, anyway? Could that be possible? Seriously? That it might, strained at her fragile composure and the fissure of fear she'd been fighting internally cracked wider, stretched and yawned like a canyon. "Buying the groceries I needed. I told you, I came over to make her dinner."

"Sir?" the uniformed officer interrupted. "Timed receipt. She was at the store at 6:10."

"So Miss Dixon is clear?" Walton pointedly asked.

"Yes, sir."

"Thanks." Walton looked back at her. "Sorry, Miss Dixon. I want to find who did this to your mother. I can't take anything for granted."

A part of her felt deeply offended, but the more practical side she used to run her jewelry store appreciated his thorough approach. "No problem." A hard lump settled in her chest. Who could have done this? What was done? "How did she . . .?" Mandy couldn't say the word out loud. Her voice failed. She ordered herself to be strong, to suck it up, and tried again. "How was my mother murdered?"

"She was shot, Miss Dixon."

"Shot?" That stunned Mandy.

"We received a shots fired call—from the neighbor. Remember?"

A shadowed memory returned. Walton telling her that the flower-lady neighbor had heard gunfire and called the police. "Yes, I remember now."

"Your mother was shot," he repeated slowly, as if realizing Mandy needed still more time to absorb and process.

She did need more time. None of this fit. It just didn't. "But my mother hated guns and forbid them in the house." Mandy looked from the crime-scene tape, twisting and crackling in the wind, back to Walton. "She must have known the person."

"Or he or she entered the house without your mother knowing it."

That was possible, and a little less terrifying. A stranger was bad, but someone you knew turning on you like that had to be worse.

"Excuse me, sir." Hank again interrupted. "May I speak to you a second?"

The detective stood up and stepped away, down to the end of the wide front porch, beyond the tall fichus, near the two white rockers. "What is it, Hank?" Walton asked, his voice carrying clearly to Mandy, still seated on the step.

"We found the point of entry in her bedroom—a window close to the corner of the house."

"Get forensics on it. Maybe we'll get lucky and pick up some prints." The detective looked over the slope of his shoulder at Mandy and elevated his voice. "Do you live here, Miss Dixon? With your mom, I mean?"

"No. I have a house on the water near my jewelry store."

"And so far as you know, no one else has been here. Just you, when you visit, and your mom."

Guilt stabbed at her. "I haven't seen anyone else here, and she hasn't mentioned anyone else being here." True, but not the whole truth. They didn't talk about her father, so she honestly didn't know if he had been here. Did he still come over every Tuesday? Mandy had no idea but, if she were a betting woman, she would bet he did. Today, however, was Thursday. From the time she was born until she had left and built her own home, she knew of no time when Charles Travest ever deviated from his scheduled Tuesday visits.

Had he deviated today?

Could he have killed her mother?

Honestly, she didn't know. Uncertainty had her again clammy and breaking into a cold sweat. He had been decent and kind to her mother and to her, and Mandy had never seen a hint of violence in him. But he'd been always been clear. If either of them crossed his lines . . .

Lines like the one her mother had set against her marrying Tim. *It isn't just your life you're putting at risk . . .*

Oh, yes. The warning had been clear and irrevocable.

Mandy's chest grew heavy, her heart tattered and weary. She could, and probably should mention that. But she didn't dare.

Tim.

Oh, you've no idea how badly I wish I could talk to you. You'd know what to do. Tears threatened. She swallowed hard three times, trying to avoid them. *I—I don't know what to do…*

Tuesday, October 21ˢᵗ

Five days later, the coroner released the body. Mandy had made arrangements with a local funeral home and withstood, without withering, the director's surprise that there'd be no service other than graveside.

The world spun on, seemingly unchanged and without notice—as arrogant as can be to someone heartbroken and mourning—and the sun shone and laughter flowed, grating at her eyes and ears and every frayed nerve in her body. For everyone else, it was a normal, largely unremarkable day.

For Mandy it was terrifying.

Little memories of her mother ran like film loops through her mind. Last week, last month, her childhood. Regardless of what she did, they wouldn't turn off. She considered going to the jewelry store to work, but she couldn't think; she'd only be in the way. Her assistant manager, Erin, had things well in hand there, so Mandy stayed home.

She'd spent years dreaming of her business and more years building it, but today she honestly couldn't care less about it. It, or anything else. Grief ruled, and ravaged and tormented her. Too weakened to fight it, she curled up on the sofa in her bathrobe with a box of tissues and let herself grieve. She had no one now. No one who cared if she lived or died. No one for her to care about or to share triumphs or troubles. No one to comfort her and assure her that no matter how dark things were now, they wouldn't always be dark.

This too shall pass. She tried comforting herself.

It rang hollow, like tin to her ears. Would it pass? Logically, she believed it would. But her heart doubted it, bombarding her with questions she didn't want to hear much less try to answer. *Is this all there really is to life? If so, why bother?*

Aching, lost, Mandy cried until she had no more tears, then cried some more. And long after the arrogant sun set for the day and the pink streaks in the sky faded to deep blue, she lay curled on her sofa, hugging the box of tissues, half of which lay wadded on the coffee table. *Help me find my way. Can you just please help me find my way?*

The following Friday, Mandy stood on the outskirts of Maddsen Cemetery at her mother's graveside. She'd always said that's where she wanted to be buried.

It was a picturesque small cemetery, very peaceful and shaded by huge, old oaks. Fresh flowers always sprinkled the graves; Mandy had seen them many times when driving by.

Thunder rumbled overhead.

It wasn't supposed to rain today so no tent stood stretched above the coffin to protect it or mourners from the weather. It sat in the open above the gaping hole prepared to receive it once the service was done.

In the distance, lightning flashed. The faint scent of it carried on the wind. The minister she'd hired reacted accordingly and spoke faster, but not fast enough. Mid-service, the sky split open and rain poured down, pinging against the top and sides of the coffin, spitting droplets that pounded the flowers placed on its top. Water gathered among the leaves and spilled over, running in rivulets down the coffin's coppery sides and dripping off into the gaping hole.

God was mourning with her.

The thought oddly comforted Mandy, and she opened her umbrella, held it over herself and the minister. Between intermittent claps of thunder and jagged streaks and flashes of lightning, she listened to him lay her mother's body to rest.

When he was done, she couldn't recall a word he'd said. Over and again in her mind, she'd remembered herself as a child playing wedding with her mother. Her mother at the piano, playing the Wedding March, while Mandy walked down a makeshift aisle of throw-rugs with a scarf-draped lampshade on her head. Her mother always added an extra note at the end of the chorus. They'd giggled about it so many times. *It's my signature note, darling . . .*

The minister claimed her attention. "I'm so sorry for your loss, Miss Dixon. Is there anything I can do for you?"

Pity burned in his eyes. Pity and curiosity that she'd stood alone to bury her mother.

She'd covertly notified Charles Travest of her mother's passing, and until she had stood through the service with only her and the minister present, she had believed her father would be here. Not that he'd said he would, but because he loved her mother. She'd even held out a glimmer of hope that, while he wouldn't live his life with his daughter, he would at least mourn her mother's passing with her. Yet, he had failed them again. One more time in a long list of times.

Oh, Mandy had sensed him nearby. Somewhere in the distant shadows watching the service. But he hadn't risked actually coming to the service or showing his face. *Coward.*

Cowardly, yes, and unfortunately typical for him. He hadn't phoned, emailed, or even sent her mother flowers with an impersonal note. No one had. The lone bouquet on top of the casket, Mandy had ordered. A white rose in her hand was the only other flower for her mother.

A tidal wave of new resentment washed over Mandy, partnered with the old. She steeled herself against its weight, lifted her chin, and then answered the minister. "No, there's nothing to be done, but thank you. I'm fine on my own."

She placed the rose onto her mother's coffin with a loving stroke, and then turned and walked away.

Safely in her car, she blotted the rain from her face and arms with a tissue, then drove off . . . and cried all the way home, shedding the tears she hadn't permitted herself to shed at the service.

Why couldn't she cry? Would that be so awful—to cry at your own mother's funeral?

Maybe not for ordinary people. But they were not ordinary. Her mother wouldn't approve the absence of emotional control; she never had. But even if she didn't disapprove this time, under these circumstances, she would need to know Mandy would be all right without her as much as Mandy needed to know her mother was all right now that she'd passed. Tears would rock her mother's confidence. Mandy couldn't do that. She wanted to imagine her mother resting in peace, not worried sick her daughter was a basket case.

That night, alone on her backyard deck, Mandy sat staring at the phone used only for secure conversations between Tim and her. Since dusk, she'd picked it up and put it back down on the little wooden side table a thousand times. Once, she'd even dialed him. Well, all but the last number. Then her mother's warning came rushing back, kicking in, and Mandy had set the phone down and had not touched it again.

Now, she fell to temptation and reached for it. She wouldn't call Tim, but she would send him a text message. He was free to respond or not without a direct confrontation. She could live with that—and if she didn't talk to someone, she was surely going to lose what was left of her mind. No one was safer or more trustworthy than Tim Branson.

Still, her heart beat hard and fast. She keyed in the text then stared at it a long moment. Her hands shook, her pulse throbbed in her throat, her head. *Please, don't let this be a mistake. Please . . .*

Before she could second-guess herself yet again or let fear back her down and force her to change her mind, she quickly pushed Send.

AUTHOR'S NOTE

I introduced the Shadow Watcher team in the Crossroad Crisis Center series. *Forget Me Not* is first story featuring Benjamin Brandt, the owner of the center. Lisa and Mark's story is *Deadly Ties*. And Joe and Beth's story is *Not This Time*.

The Shadow Watchers play significant roles in *Not This Time*. Readers requested more of their stories, so I wrote *The Marked Bride*.

That left two more team members needing *Shadow Watcher* books. I couldn't leave out Nick or Sam!

Both of those books are now available. Nick's story is *The Marked Star* and Sam's is *The Marked Witness.*

Nick is definitely out of his element when he's asked to help find the grown daughter of a man he's worked with before—the CEO of a weaponry firm. NINA wants the weapons, and they've taken his daughter, a famous singer named Elle, hostage. Nick and Elle are an unlikely match, but those are often the most fun.

Sam said he would, and indeed he did send me on a merry chase in *The Marked Witness.* His isn't the story I planned for him, but it is the story he insisted was his, so there it is. I just followed along and noted what I observed, and I have to tell you, his *real* story is better than my imagined one! There's something compelling about Sam and the way he reacts toward a child and that child reacts to him that makes his story one of my all-time favorites.

Thank you for your emails and letters and reviews. Without them, after including the first Shadow Watchers in the Crossroads Crisis Center series, I might not have written these **Shadow Watcher** books, and I'm so very glad I did. I enjoy the team very much and love the way they interact with one another!

These three stories wrap up the Shadow Watcher series, but I don't know if I can resist doing this type of story again, so in the future the lure of visiting Seagrove Village again might be too much for me to overcome. There is Omega One and his team to consider. They've been very much in the shadows and we might just have to see if they'll step into the light so we can dip into their lives.

Do share your thoughts on that. And, as always, thank you for reading!

Blessings,
Vicki

P.S. I also invite you to subscribe to my author newsletter so when I have new releases, you'll be the first to know.

ABOUT THE AUTHOR

VICKI HINZE is the author of nearly fifty novels, nonfiction books and hundreds of articles published in more than sixty-three countries. Her books have received many prestigious awards and nominations, including her selection for *Who's Who in the World* (as a writer and educator), nominations for Career Achievement and Reviewer's Choice Awards for Best Series and Suspense Storyteller of the Year, Best Romantic Suspense Storyteller of the Year and Best Romantic Intrigue Novel of the Year. She co-created an innovative, open-ended continuity series of single-title romance novels, an innovative suspense series, and has helped to establish sub-genres in military women's fiction (suspense and intrigue and action and adventure) and in military romantic-thriller novels. Hinze loves genre-blending and blazing new trails for readers and other authors. She is a former columnist for Social-In Global Network and radio host of *Everyday Woman.*

Get Vicki's monthly newsletter at **http://mad.ly/ signups/82943/join**

ALSO BY VICKI HINZE

Behind Closed Doors: Family Secrets

Blood Strangers

StormWatch Series

Deep Freeze

Bringing Home Christmas

Clean Read

S.A.S.S. Unit Series

Black Market Body Double | The Sparks Broker | The Mind Thief | Operation Stealing Christmas | S.A.S.S. Confidential

Clean Read

Breakdown Series

so many secrets | her deepest fear (Short Read)

Down and Dead, Inc. Series

Down and Dead in Dixie | Down and Dead in Even |

Down and Dead in Dallas

Clean Read

Shadow Watchers (Crossroads Crisis Center related)

The Marked Star | The Marked Bride | The Marked Witness | Wed to Death: A Shadow Watchers Short

Clean Reads

Crossroads Crisis Center Series

Forget Me Not | Deadly Ties | Not This Time

Clean Read Inspirational

The Reunion Collection

Her Perfect Life | Mind Reader | Duplicity |
Clean Reads

Lost, Inc.

Survive the Night | Christmas Countdown |
Torn Loyalties
Clean Read Inspirational

War Games Series

Body Double | Double Vision | Double Dare | Smokescreen: Total Recall
| Kill Zone
General Audience (out of print)

The Lady Duo

Lady Liberty | Lady Justice
General Audience

Military

Shades of Gray | Acts of Honor | All Due Respect
General Audience

Paranormal Romantic Suspense

Legend of the Mist | Maybe This Time
General Audience

Seascape Novels

Beyond the Misty Shore | Upon a Mystic Tide |
Beside a Dreamswept Sea
General Audience

Other

Girl Talk: Letters Between Friends **|** My Imperfect Valentine | Invitation to a Murder | Bulletproof | The Madonna Key (series co-creator) | Before the White Rose | Invidia

Multiple-Author Collections

Dangerous Desires | My Evil Valentine | Risky Brides | Smart Women and Dangerous Men | Christmas Heroes | Love is Murder | Cast of Characters | A Message from Cupid Seeing Fireworks

Nonfiction Books

In Case of Emergency: What You Need to Know When I Can't Tell You | One Way to Write a Novel | Writing in the Fast Lane | All About Writing to Sell |

Mistakes Writers Make and How-To Avoid Them

For a complete listing visit http://vickihinze.com/books